# MALE AND FEMALE

# MALE AND FEMALE

JACK WOODFORD

CUTTING EDGE

ISBN-13: 978-1-970848-16-8

Published by
Cutting Edge Books
PO Box 8212
Calabasas, CA 91372
www.cuttingedgebooks.com

# CHAPTER ONE

## *TWO DAYS MORE OF*
## *INNOCENCE*

COOLLY NAKED, Elaine stood by the curtained window, looking down into the tennis court below.

Hyde was there waiting. He was what girls spoke of as a "Magnificent Male Specimen."

She studied him in the deep perplexity that had come to her concerning him of late. He was wearing white duck pants and white tennis shoes.... A thick, black belt. White silk shirt, open at the throat; sleeves cut short.

There were bulges of muscle at his forearms. When he stooped to retrieve a tennis ball his trousers tightened against his thighs and she saw the muscles of his straight, strong legs tauten. He was superbly balanced and symmetrical; not enough muscle to be bulgy; sufficient to make for strong, masculine suppleness and agility.

Throwing a tennis ball into the air he caught it dexterously upon his racket. For a moment his face was upturned.... Sun on it. Handsome? God yes, she thought, he was splendid. Direct blue eyes. Brownish hair. Crinkly. Shiny.

Then why should she—?

Puckering pencil-line brows she pondered. Two days more and she would be married to Hyde, who waited now, below, to play tennis with her.

... Two days more and she'd be in bed with him.... Unreservedly in his arms. She! ... A virgin.... Who had never known the ultimate male caress.

Then why—? she asked herself vaguely—

... Certainly there was no other man in her mind or heart. Nor had there ever been. Male pals ... in high school, even grammar school ... at college.... Of course these had usually tried to make love to her; but she'd discouraged it because—well, why *had* she discouraged it, she wondered?

She'd accepted Hyde.... So that was *that*. Not that it had been *wholly* a matter of expedience because of her father's financial dilemmas and Hyde's money.

... Of course that *had* figured in it, to a certain extent.... But she honestly *did* like him.... Always had. More than any other man—till now.... Now that she knew she must soon marry him.... Now she nearly hated him.... Was being purposely dilatory because she didn't want even to play tennis with him.... Now that their association had changed from a loosely general one to a definitely specific one.

Walking over to the mirror she examined her reflection. What, she inwardly interrogated, ailed her anyway? ... Twenty-four. Intelligent beyond the average. Apparently quite normal.

Gazing down at her creamy soft pink white person she inventoried herself with a new acuteness of perception.

Small satiny half globes, tipped with daintiest pink. Rounded shoulders and gracile, tapering arms. A small throat. Strikingly pretty oval face, with large, blue eyes, piquant, provocative, slightly damp lips. Corn colored hair, luxurious and plentiful but composed of thinnest, finest individual strands.

Narrow hips and slender, ideally proportioned thighs.... An instrument of passion so perfect for its obviously intended purposes as to impress even its feminine possessor. For what purpose, she argued, could she have been given this cream and pink warm soft body except ...

There had been no real reason for a bath at this time of day she realized guiltily.... Just another effort on her part to delay seeing Hyde ... like many another such gesture since their engagement. She remembered his kisses that night.... Firm masculine mouth over hers; pressing down so hard that she felt his china-like even teeth.... Strong, possessive, man arms around her, straining her to him. Desire for her beating through his body like a tocsin full of strange new alarms. How he would like to get his hands on her ... after a marriage license gave him full leave to!

... And why, she asked herself, wouldn't she like it too? What was wrong?

Still delaying before putting on her clothes she went to the dressing table. Perfumed her body at intimate points, though there was certainly no necessity for scenting young femininity richly equipped with fragrance naturally attractive to the male. Taking up a large body powder puff she dipped it into a huge tin of powder and, dusting herself liberally, turned her person into a fleshly bonbon.

She reflected, as she rubbed the powder in with her hands, that all her softness was to be crushed in hard, hairy masculine arms. Kissed, caressed in passionate transports.

Could she go through with it, she asked herself? Suppose, she reflected, after the marriage, she couldn't possibly ... and Hyde was such a good sort ... so deserving of everything a man might expect in marriage.

She moved again to the window. Her mother and father were away. The servants, she realized, would think nothing of Hyde's coming upstairs. Why not? Wasn't it better for his interests as well as for her own to find out first whether—raising the window she called through the curtain. His face turned up eagerly.

"Are you ever coming down here, Elaine?"

"Come up here a minute, Hyde."

He walked toward the house.

# CHAPTER TWO
## *EXPERIMENT IN TEMPTATION*

THERE WERE windows on two sides of the room. Beyond the windows trees. Through the trees, at one point, a vista of the ocean.

It was a soft, creamy room; impregnated with the fragrance of intimate femininity. The bed was of wood, covered with a rich, cream enamel.

Hyde paused, just inside the door, arrested by a sense of confusion that he couldn't precisely define. It was the sort of room in which a strong, wholly masculine man would be a trifle ill at ease; though not, necessarily, in an unpleasant sense.

"… Well—come in—Hyde—I won't bite you."

"The servants?"

"… To hell with them."

"O. K. with me, Elaine, if you don't care."

"I don't."

Still uneasy and a trifle gauche he slumped into a chair and let his racket drop to the floor. One of his pockets bulged with a tennis ball. His presence, she felt with irritation, was violating. So far as she could recall, no man had ever before been in her room.… Well, she corrected, no real *man*. The servants were equipped with an impersonality which removed them to a limbo of sexlessness.

Sunshine was in him still, as though he had soaked it up. Mixed emotions made her mind such a chaos that she could adduce nothing coherent. There was an awkward pause.

Picking up a light blue silk boudoir gown she wrapped it around her.... Felt an odd impulse to pull it more tightly around her. After a moment he said:

"What's the big idea? I've been waiting for more than half an hour."

She exhaled a cloud of blue cigarette smoke.

"Don't feel like playing tennis today."

"Well, why didn't you say so then, instead of—say, Elaine, what's gotten into you lately? You're so darned different."

She crossed shapely legs. Several days before, while in town, she'd bought a book.... Carried it in her hand along Fifth Avenue. In the book, as though it had been hollow, she'd felt the vibrations of heavy traffic passing on the street. Something of the sort she felt within her now.

"Not going to start quarreling with me *before* marriage, Hyde—!"

He plainly evidenced surprise.

" 'Quarrel with you—' Hardly! Where'd you get that idea?"

"You seem provoked."

"... Well, after all, I've been waiting nearly an hour for you to—"

"Yes, I know." She let her attention wander from him to the window, with a far-away expression. Yet though abstracted she was also acutely conscious of him.... Knew that he was devouring her with his eyes. Every detail. More and more she could feel the sensation of vibration coming from him. It filled the room. She was aware that her negligee had a trifle fallen away from one shoulder, and that a bare, ivory-like expanse of rounded, warm flesh was visible. She could feel his eyes feast upon the bare flesh almost as hotly as though it were actually his lips which touched her. Her body was still bath warmed and on it was the fragrance of the bath salts she had used; she knew that he was aware of all this. She even experienced a certain pleasure in being aware that the knowledge caused him extreme discomfort.

"Elaine!"

It was a sharp exclamation from him. She turned inquiring eyes upon him. But he did not say more; only stared at her, fixedly, like a sleep walker. She saw his nostrils dilate as he drew in sharp breaths and exhaled shortly. When he was excited his hair slipped back a trifle, as his scalp moved. One of his strong hands was upon his knee. She saw that he was tense. The muscles in his hand stood out like whipcord.

Slowly he rose. Moved toward her. She watched him, fascinated, trembling. He stopped before her. Stood gazing down at her fixedly. From where he stood now she knew that he could see the beginning rise of her firm young breasts beneath the flimsy blue gown.

"Elaine, why did you send for me?"

She did not answer. He dropped to his knees before her. Put his arms around her. Pressed his lips to the warm-soft powdered flesh of her rounded shoulder.... And then he grew bolder. Disarranged her negligee. His mouth dwelt upon the softness of her flesh. She took a sharp breath.

"Elaine ... I'm mad about you. You ought not to have sent for me like this. Until after ... do you think I'm made of ... I'd better go—I—Oh Elaine ... if you only knew how I've wanted to—" she listened acutely and in something approaching offense, as though she were hearing a dread confession. She hoped he would go on. He did.

"... I never let you see how I felt before ... because.... Well, because there's something strange about you. You don't like to be cuddled like other girls. I was afraid if I let you know how much I wanted you, you'd—Oh, I don't know how to say it, only I—"

He ceased talking now, and boldly disarranged more of her negligee. Picked her up.... Carried her across the room. Put her down. There was no more negligee. She shut her eyes. There was no sound save that of his heavy breathing and the faint sound of birds in the garden below. His lips on her sensate skin. Touching it lightly here; pressing down there. Bolder and bolder.

She struggled. His strong arms were around her tightly. She could not escape. His mouth down over hers. She felt bruised and humiliated.

"Don't!—Don't! *Don't!*" she wailed. Her tone, rather than her words, penetrated deeply into his consciousness. He released her.

"Elaine ... I'm sorry ... but you are so desirable—"

"There's nothing to be sorry about, Hyde; it was my fault. I called you up here."

She saw that he would not be coherent so long as he contemplated her revealed loveliness. Men were—she struggled to define the thing in her mind but could not. Instead she hurriedly rearranged the sleazy boudoir gown. When this was done he appeared to have gained control. She watched while he made himself presentable.... And when he had done so she felt a complete change come over her.

She liked him that way. Her old warmth toward him returned. He sat down, dejected, and she pulled a chair near to him so that she could speak to him in a low tone.

"Never mind, Hyde; I tell you it was all my fault."

"Can you ever forgive me, Elaine?"

"There's nothing to forgive; you didn't do anything."

"I know, but I was going to. I don't know what came over me."

"Don't be silly, Hyde; can't you see that it was *all* my fault."

"But why, Elaine—why did you send for me to come up here?" '

"It's hard to explain ... you see, I—Hyde, are you quite sure that you want to marry me?"

"Of *course* I'm sure. It's you who—"

"I don't know if I love you, Hyde; I don't know if there *is* anything, really, in 'love.' But I do like you, a lot. Really I do. And there's certainly no one else. Never has been—and I don't think there ever could be. But do you think we ought to marry, considering the fact that I may not be able to go through with—"

He took both of her tiny, smooth hands in his larger, strong ones. Said earnestly:

"Elaine, if there could *never* be *that* between us I'd still love you and want to marry you."

"Oh, it isn't a question of never, Hyde. I may have to wait a bit till I get over ... goodness knows what. That's why I sent for you, to see if I—well, I failed.... Aren't you afraid that ours may not be a happy marriage?"

"No, because I'll be ever so patient and considerate. I'll wait until you—"

"I'll try to be all you want me to be, Hyde."

"You don't have to try. You were born everything I want you to be."

"Well, then, let's forget all this. Go on back to the tennis court. I'll be there in a few minutes."

"You do forgive me then, Elaine?"

"... It was all my fault, Hyde."

He patted her clumsily upon the shoulder. She saw that he was pale and shaken. He went on out of the room and she heard him descending the stairs slowly, as though he were in deep thought.

She put on panties and a brassiere. Reached for a sweater and a skirt, still considering what had passed between them.... The experiment, she concluded, had yielded totally negative results.

What, she asked herself, was wrong? The invitations for the wedding were all out. She must go through with the ceremony. Her father had been so happy at her decision—arrived at partly through her mother's tactful urging—to marry Hyde.... And she had never wished to marry any man ... probably never would, she felt; so why not Hyde, since, apparently it would make everyone concerned, except herself, happy—and it would not make her too desperately unhappy. She would manage to go through with the whole aspect of marriage, eventually.... She'd simply have to, she assured herself—even if it—she gripped the edge of her dressing table, as her mind developed clear pictures.... But, after all, she questioned, why not? ... Any other girl would be—!

Her eyes went to a picture upon the dressing table.... The photograph of a strikingly beautiful girl with dark, intense eyes, raven black hair; and, Elaine knew, skin like whitest alabaster. A sensitivity akin to the vibration she had felt coming from Hyde went through her.

# CHAPTER THREE
## LOVE-NEST IN MANHATTAN

H E HADN'T previously, Hyde now saw, considered love and marriage very seriously.

Now that he did come to think about it, he found that there were, roughly bundled together in his mind, a number of correlated speculations, none of them of any real use.

Many people, he was certain, married for no more than purely fleshly reasons. Even though they did not usually realize that they were so actuated, the realization, he felt, came to them as a distinct shock when they had found that their interest in each other waned after repeated physical contacts.

... But it couldn't be that, he assured himself, in respect to Elaine and himself. *That* was *different*. Quite different from everything that had gone before—and much had gone before.

Now that he looked back upon what had gone before he felt that practically all of it had been meaningless, save as it had contributed to a process of elimination facing life's possibilities. He had eliminated, it would now seem, everything except the joys of a happy marriage ... companionship with a congenial woman ... children. Yes, it would be nice to be a father; that, indeed, would be a new "thrill." ... A legal father, whose offspring would be recognized by society.

He was thirty. High time that he became a parent. He would like to have a son into whom he could project himself and vicariously live again as he grew older. His son would be a football player; yes, above everything else he must play foot-ball.... And he must lead a widely colorful life during his younger years—and then he must settle down to something steady and worth while.

Hyde frowned in some perplexity, and his hair, characteristically, slipped back as he meditated.

The address of his small apartment near Columbia University was unknown even to his parents—he had rented the place under an assumed name so that he would have a sanctuary to which he might flee when he wished to be alone.

In the apartment building he was known only as a young man taking some graduate work toward a Ph.D. at Columbia. Because of the vast anonymity of New York no one of his friends, relatives or acquaintances had ever discovered his retreat.

He had supposed that it would not be long before someone discovered his little apartment; passed the word along to others, and hence into the gossip columns of the newspapers, where, not seldom, he was commented upon, usually with a friendly jocularity, since he knew most of the town columnists and had long been recognized as a thoroughly "good fellow" in all quarters. But it had been nearly a year now, and nobody had discovered his cozy acropolis.

The building was a huge one, containing several hundred small apartments. At the building entrance was a doorman in wine-colored livery. The lobby was a bit florid, being furnished with the imitation antique cabinets, combined with modern overstuffed furniture, that represent a New York apartment building proprietor's delusions of grandeur.

Just beyond the building was the "Valley," inhabited by many Spaniards and Mexicans, on the edge of Harlem. From his windows Hyde could see far out over the congested valley. It was a view which interested him far more than the placid one from the windows of his rooms at home on Long Island.

His "hideaway" was on the fifteenth floor of the buildings ... Down a long hall and around a bend in the hall. Just before the elevators in the hall was a vividly yellow couch where tenants sat when waiting for the elevators; aside from this one touch, the hallway had an institutional air, with its tiled floor. white walls, and black doors, which had apartment numbers painted upon them in gold.

There was a pleasant blankness about these doors. He had never seen any of them open or shut; never seen anyone enter or leave them. Usually his arrivals and departures were at odd hours.

Inside his apartment was a short entryway, off of which were a kitchenette, equipped with an electric stove, and an automatic ice box and also a roomy clothes closet. There was a living room and bedroom. In the living room he kept, of his own possessions, only a few books and two favorite pipes.

The bathroom opened off of the bedroom; and on the bathroom door was a mirror which reflected everything that went on in the bedroom.

Tonight Hyde was glad of the apartment. He wanted to see no one.... Wanted to try to straighten out his thoughts.

... That scene with Elaine, in her bedroom. What in Heaven's name could it possibly mean, he speculated.

He searched back over his stock of experiences, but nothing quite fitted. Or at least he would not permit it to fit where Elaine was concerned. And now that he came to survey his past with concentration, there appeared to be a startling paucity of material in it worth considering, or of use in gauging things that were of real importance.

There were the years at school; the three and a half years abroad after college; the four and a half years of sheer experimentation, including summers at various fashionable resorts and side excursions now and then up to Banff and down to Mexico.... And in and out and through all these memories the sinuous warmth and shapely fragrance of female flesh.... That, in fact, appeared to him now to be the common denominator of all his living so far. He was startled, now that he contemplated this fact; it had not before occurred to him quite so distinctly.... Yet, he was comfortably certain, he was not unusually addicted to the pleasures of the flesh; not more so than the average normal young man of wealth. Most young men, he knew, situated economically as he was, in all ages, had lived in much the same fashion.

... And after marriage, he felt quite certain, there would still be women ... other than Elaine. She was certainly not the sort to fuss about that—theirs would, of course, be a more intelligent relation than the usual middle-class marital state.

He had supposed, he recalled, that there had already been some of that sort of thing in Elaine's life ... but now, after the experience of the afternoon, he knew that he had been mistaken. She had acted like a virgin... Given every evidence of being frightened.

Brows drawn thoughtfully together he slowly paced back and forth across the floor, puffing upon a pipe.

How silly, how downright ridiculous it would be, he reflected with much perturbation, if he were in reality drawn toward her only because of her flesh. But those few minutes in her room ... with desire beating through him in a way that it seldom had before!—He shrugged.... Perhaps it had been only because of his sudden sensing of her virginal state.... But yet, previously, also, he had felt the urge and burn of desire for her flesh. Even now there was upon him, left over from the passion heat of the afternoon, an ache of fleshly desire which bid fair to make his night sleepless. He shook his head in disgust.

Was it possible, he thought anxiously, that the years of carnal living he viewed so lightly as being only those usual to the male, had in him set up a druggish sort of desire for sensual gratification that could not be so easily controlled as he had supposed?

Tonight, assuredly, it seemed that way. He glanced at the clock. It was long after midnight—and he was tired; but he could not sleep. Suppose, he conjectured, even after marriage, Elaine for some queer reason—and he sensed that there *was* a queer reason of some sort underlying—refused to give herself to him? He stopped in the middle of the floor. The very thought of such things sent a riot of heat through his blood; heat that would, he knew, drive off sleep for hours.

Now he was beginning to see why so often marriages which gave every evidence of being auspicious ones at the beginning ended messily in Reno.... Conjugal felicity was a far more complicated affair than he had supposed.... In the past he'd thought: "After a time I'll settle down and marry—have children— some pretty girl—good family—right socially... And Elaine had fitted into all that so nicely.... Yet? Obviously this afternoon she had wished to discover if they might be physically congenial; and she had discovered—what?—Well, hell, he reflected nervously, the invitations were out; all the preparations had been made.... So that was *that.* No use speculating *now.* He dragged heavily upon his pipe and his hair slipped back.

Impatiently, and with an irascibility and nervousness new to him—since he was in splendid physical and mental health—he put the pipe down and stepped to the 'phone.... One couldn't pace the floor all night, he admonished inwardly, when one was dated up for the prime event of one's life ... must get some rest.... Somehow. *Anyhow!*

Sally Tuttle was from Oklahoma City. A senior at college. He'd met her in a little restaurant on Amsterdam Avenue several weeks before. The usual sort of thing. Smiles from table to table. "Going my way ...?" That kind of *affaire*. Silly but effective. Sally was a cute little trick. And amazingly sophisticated. Slender and immature; with breasts so slight as to be almost unobservable when she was dressed; but there, nevertheless.... Narrow, boyish thighs. Softest of white skin. Dainty ... to the point of fragility. Probably, he reflected, stinted on food most of the time. Learned every sensual trick readily; looked startlingly youthful and innocent and yet was as devoid of the possibility of embarrassment as a burlesque "Fan Dancer."

A sleepy, childish falsetto came over the 'phone almost immediately after he put in a call. Hyde spoke briefly. When Sally said she'd be over in half an hour she *meant* half an hour. She was one of those singularly fortunate young women who did not have to work for an hour on her face, after rising from bed, in order to make it presentable. She was presentable at all times, even when she woke up yawning and stretching in the morning. He had always felt a trifle guilty over her. She was such a child. Yet her actions! ... And she was so surprisingly matter-of-fact. Things were cut and dried with Sally. No necessity for a pretense of love. If there were a new outfit of clothes involved, anything went—with as much expedition as possible. There would not be a moment's delay when she arrived.

Feeling infinitely better Hyde entered the bathroom and stepped under the shower. Lathered under the warm water and felt his nervous tension relax. Graduated the water to icy cold and let the needles from the spray prick away every vestige of soap.... Then a brief alcohol rub. His body glowed and throbbed. His heart hammered. The blood sang in his ears.

He had just finished his bath when he heard a soft tapping on the door.

Sally stepped into the room, looking cuddly and bed warmed. Taking her coat and hat he put them into the closet. Nonchalantly she went to a small stand and took up a cigarette. He lighted it for her.

"Lot of nerve," she chided, "getting me up this time of morning. I've got a class I can't cut at ten tomorrow."

"Don't cut it," he advised; "cut one of the afternoon classes, so you can go shopping."

Here large, dark baby eyes glowed, not with the usual avariciousness of a New York gold digger, but with the delight of a naïve child who knew that on the morrow she could go shopping in dead earnest, not just window shopping.

Though thoroughly acquiescent in all matters, there were some toward which she showed, naturally, more reluctance than others. Hyde said:

"This time you can have a whole outfit. A new dress *and* trimmings ... shoes ... stockings ... some underwear ... a new hat."

She gasped.

"All that! Gee!"

Hyde sat down in one of the comfortable, overstuffed chairs. It was built low, and one naturally slid far forward in it.

"Come here," he directed. She glanced nervously at the light switch. He shook his head.

"Leave it on, if you please."

After a moment he broke in with:

"No. Wait."

Rising he turned off the switch. Resumed his seat. It was inky dark in the apartment. Resolution surged through him.... The other considerations would have to be minor ones: ... Smug married respectability. Children. Elaine! The thought of her; of her lips, her daintiness … her fragile blonde allure, was upon him like a fever. Elaine had everything … all the desirability of any woman he had ever enjoyed; and, something vastly more than that too. An air of the patrician…. She was, in the strictest interpretation of the word, "a lady." There was something particularly and unusually vivifying about the thought of a lady becoming as intimate with one, irr dalliance, as those casual pretty creatures whom one naturally subjected to the extremes of sensual pleasure.

… To think of Elaine thus submitting—he'd do it—force her—no matter what—despite her reluctance, shame, *anything!*…

Now, fully, he recognized the truth of his previous, tentative supposition. Not exempt from the usual human weaknesses, his years of voluptuous living *had* accustomed him beyond all weaning to the use of the sweetest of human drugs.

# CHAPTER FOUR
## *WHY SHOULDN'T*
## *I MARRY HIM?*

THE MAIDS annoyed her; Elaine had dismissed them. She'd been trying on things all day. Endless bits of lingerie; stockings, new dresses, were all over the large room, and in the next room just off her bedroom.

It was about four-thirty. Her father was somewhere downstairs, doubtless reading and rereading the stock market section of the evening paper; an occupation which had, as long as she could recall, caused him more displeasure than everything else in the world put together. Yet stoically he persisted in subjecting himself. Her mother would doubtless be telephoning. Calling up people was one of her chief joys in life.

Tired, she went to one of the windows. It was a gray day outside. A discouraging sort of day.... The kind which prompted one to reflect without optimism upon the eventualities of life. It was, she thought, one of the grayest days that she had ever seen.

She felt that a radical change was coming over the whole complexion of her life.... So far it had been an easy one.... School ... social affairs ... mild flirtations ... buying clothes ... wearing them ... going to the right summering places, both in America and abroad. Dabbling a bit in art; learning to identify the various modern movements. Miriam was a good hand at that sort of thing. *Miriam....* The memory that she was coming over caused Elaine to have a slight sense of lift, which evaporated when she remembered Hyde.

Indignation filled her, for, so far as she could learn by inward scrutiny, no good reason. Usually, before, she had thought of Hyde only with pleasure. She thought back to their meeting, some years before.... When he had been an end, for Yale.... That magnificent Thanksgiving Day in New Haven, and the party that had followed ... Hyde had been so smooth, so *right....* Not at all the obvious, pawing kind. But now that she knew he wanted her body.... Damn it! She stamped a tiny, slipper-clad foot in fury.

A child! Her dainty, fragile body. Was *that* all it was good for! Strange, she reflected, that she had never contemplated such matters before. But there had always been protection ... from everything. Years in school had been an efficient protection from thinking or from learning to think.

Her social and economic status had been protection against the predatory advances of completely unscrupulous males.... They hinted mildly and sometimes pawed a bit, when one was in the social register; but, for their more forthright campaigns they used young actresses, even waitresses, or the daughters of men not so fortunately situated, socially and economically, as her father.

And more than that, she thoroughly realized now for the first time, there had been an unusual protective device of some sort within her own consciousness; a device not general among young ladies of her age. She had never been emotionally disturbed by any man, so there had not been in her experience the hectic flareups which had occurred in the lives of most of her feminine friends—with the exception, of course, of Miriam. Miriam, Elaine decided, was not cold, but she was reserved, and had an excellent sense of good and bad taste.

Beyond the windows there was a light mist which blew in from the ocean. When she looked at open spaces beyond the window the mist was not observable; but when she looked directly at a stationary object, like a tree, she could see the mist moving past in ghostly fashion. She remembered something she had read in connection with one of her studies, concerning vast stellar accumulations of such mists, floating around the universe. Some day the world might encounter one of these drifting mists and remain in it for a long time. Should this happen, all life on earth would suffer some queer change, because of an interference with the sun's rays.

It was like that, she felt, now, with her. This queer mist of marriage and men had been floating near her orbit of existence for years, and she had been more or less blithely unaware of it. Now she was moving into it; and her life.... Of course, she reasoned, it would be possible to avoid the whole matter in several ways. If she went downstairs now and flatly refused to marry Hyde tomorrow there would be a scene. Her father would grumble; her mother would exhibit a convincing case of hysteria. Hyde would be annoyed. People would gossip, but the whole matter would die down in a few weeks or months. Other girls in her station in life had done much the same sort of thing. It would be nothing new.

... No, she decided, the far easier solution was to go ahead and marry; with divorce later, if necessary.... And, besides, it would be silly to go on unmarried. It was high time—and—Hyde would be considered an ideal husband by—

Miriam entered without knocking. Elaine turned toward her and, without speaking, examined her curiously. Miriam, in her rich contralto, inquired:

"... Well, what's the quizzical expression for?"

"... Nothing, Miriam."

"You never gave me such a once-over as *that* before!"

" ... Oh, you appear to be so—so—well, it's rotten outside, and one would think you had just come in from a bright, sun-shiny day, and—"

Miriam made a mock bow and sat down, throwing one shapely limb over the other.

"It *is* disagreeable out today."

"... And in...." Elaine added lugubriously.

"Why! What's wrong, Elaine?"

Miriam waited; but Elaine, still standing by the window, said nothing further.

Miriam was pleasantly conscious of appearing well. She usu-ally did. She never curled or artificially arranged her smooth black hair. She parted it in the middle and combed it straight back on either side of her well-shaped head, winding it into a tight knot at the back.

She was wearing a smartly tailored black suit, and a small, jaunty black hat. There was about her, as usual, the striking impression of whiteness, but her cheeks were healthily and natu-rally colored.

Miriam, Elaine knew, used very little make-up. Her dark brows were plucked to slim pencil lines, but her naturally dark lashes needed no touching up. Her lips were so vividly red that they appeared to have been touched with lip carmine; but they had not been; the contrast of her white skin accentuated their natural redness.

Smaller than Elaine, she was well balanced and nicely propor-tioned; not, however, reflecting the Grecian standard of symmetry. Her hips were narrow and boylike.... Slender, lithe limbs and arms and splendidly rounded shoulders. Despite her slight stature she exhibited a strength and firmness not usual to women.

When Elaine did not reply, Miriam rose and went over to put an arm around her affectionately:

"You're obviously not happy. I have noticed it before, but I thought it was just a temporary case of nerves; it isn't, is it? Tell me, what's—"

Elaine shook her head. Moved across the room. Sat down upon the bed. Remained in that position for a moment, and then with a troubled sigh lay back, full length, upon the bed, her arms arched above her head; staring unhappily at the ceiling.

"What is it, Elaine; surely you can tell *me*."

For several moments Elaine did not reply.

"Yes, Miriam, I could tell you. I would tell you—if I knew what it is—but I don't, precisely."

"What do you mean, dear?"

"That's just it—I don't know."

"Don't you *want* to marry Hyde?"

"No."

Miriam felt herself suddenly exhilarated. Her fear fled; she felt suddenly lifted, exultant.

"Well, then, my dear, why *do* you marry him?"

"Why shouldn't I?"

"Have you discovered something of which you weren't aware when you became engaged?"

"Nothing of any great significance, I guess."

"Elaine, is there money involved in this; did your father—?"

"It's not that crude, quite. There is some reason why the marriage will benefit Dad, I don't know just what it is. There was no urging.... Not on his part anyway."

"Then your mother—?"

"Oh, of course, socially, she's gone on the idea, but—well, she wouldn't carry the thing so far as to insist. I could back out if I wanted to."

"You don't want to?"

Instead of answering the question Elaine asked one:

"Have you ever had an *affaire* with a man, Miriam? We never discussed those things much, did we?"

"No, we didn't." Miriam gazed down at her knees, thinking furiously. "And I've never had an *affaire* with a man. Petting, necking ... had them trying their damndest, all that sort of thing, but—"

"Miriam, men are hard and hairy and bony, and they—"

Miriam was startled, but she found herself replying in a low, troubled tone:

"Yes, I know, Elaine, but Hyde is a man, and in two days you'll be married to him."

"I know," Elaine went on, "it's not the way one ought to feel. I like Hyde. I honestly do. But, damn it, Miriam.... He practically tried to rape me."

Miriam sprang up, her lovely dark eyes blazing.

"Why the—!"

"Wait, you don't understand. I put him up to it to see whether ... it wasn't his fault at all. He was mighty decent about it. He couldn't have been blamed for anything he might have done, under the circumstances, since I—"

Miriam sat down again and fought for control. Said dully:

"I see—you couldn't wait."

Elaine raised herself on one elbow and stared at her friend, puzzled by her tone.

"You don't understand at all, Miriam; it wasn't that—I haven't the least desire for that kind of contact with a man— never have had—and now I think I've found out that I never will have."

Miriam exulted inwardly, and said:

"Then—?"

"... And I'm going to promise to love, honor and obey him, Miriam. Is it fair to Hyde?"

"What did he say after, after the—?"

"He blamed himself, of course—and he is willing to take the chance—the chance that after we're married things will straighten out."

"And you—?" the question was whispered by Miriam.

"Well, I think I had better go ahead and take the chance too. If there were any other man; if there ever had been, if there were ever likely to be ... but, since things are as they are I suppose the best thing to do is to go ahead with the marriage and try to get over being silly."

"Yes, Elaine, I guess that's best." As she spoke Miriam sat up and examined her fingers attentively, but without seeing them or being conscious of what she was doing. Inwardly, her mind was racing, reveling in the hopes which were being reborn as Elaine spoke.

She had wanted Hyde for herself, but not as a man. The idea of physical love between a man and a woman repelled her, filled her with a nauseating disgust that knew no bounds. To her, Hyde was not a man, but a symbol of the only things in life she cared about; wealth, influence, and power. She despised her precarious place in the rich, smart set of which she, Elaine and Hyde were members. The family wealth was dissipating rapidly through the incompetent hands of her mother, who seemed hopelessly unaware of the world about her. Miriam's fingers were now on the bottom rung of the ladder, and Elaine was her only friend in this snobbish, predatory group. They were all waiting with grim anticipation for the inevitable time when she would lose her grip. She had made a frantic bid for Hyde as a last chance to get to the top of that ladder, where she could trample on all of their fingers and watch them slip at her pleasure into the same oblivion and doom that they had so passionately wished for her.

Hyde had eluded her, however, with an uncanny male perception that told him her ardor was born of desperation and not affection. He had sensed her hard coldness, her unfeminine ruthlessness, and had turned to Elaine for the qualities she lacked and could not feign. And now! Miriam exulted, Elaine herself, his warm, cuddly Elaine has confessed the same abhorrence of the idea of becoming his wife in the physical sense that had kept her from winning him! She gloried in the immense possibilities of the situation. There could be no real happiness between them as long as Elaine felt this way, and Miriam decided with a grim determination that she would never change. She would seize upon and nurture this emotional infirmity of Elaine's until it grew like an evil weed and choked the very life from the marriage. Her mind searched feverishly for her next step.

There was a long pause. They could faintly hear the wind blowing the slight fog in from the sea. The silence within the room became so acute that they both distinctly heard the faint tick of a French clock on Elaine's dressing table.

"There's one more thing I'd like to find out, Miriam; it may explain everything … explain why I've never … why you've never…." Miriam sat very still. It seemed to her that her whole body became still … that her heart stopped beating, and her blood stopped flowing through her veins. Elaine ceased speaking, and the silence in the room again became acute and unbearable; on the landing outside a deep-toned chime clock struck the half hour.

"No man will ever touch me again, Elaine."

"Again? You mean?"

Miriam nodded significantly. Her mind raced on ahead of the lie which was already falling from her lips.

"When I was only twelve," Miriam said, "a cousin who was already a young man tried to bother me while we were reading in my bedroom. After he found out that I was still too young for that purpose, he decided to try something else."

Miriam watched with an evil delight as Elaine's face turned pale at the sickening details she composed.

# CHAPTER FIVE
## *A COCKTAIL WITH THE CHAUFFEUR*

I
T WAS A "quiet" wedding.

In the Bronx it would have been considered a magnificent one; but in the little Long Island church, with only friends and acquaintances attending, it was, considering the social and economic positions of the families, not an extraordinarily florid affair. For one thing, it was an out-of-season wedding; and for another, both families fondly supposed themselves to be handling the whole matter very economically—though Sally Tuttle would have been struck dumb with awe.

... Not that there was any great necessity for economy. The major parties concerned were merely suffering from a bad case of frozen assets; which would come to life gloriously again "when, as, and if," as the investment bankers worded it, the country's financial status improved.

Miriam, dressed in white, with her vivid coloration, was no less impressive than the bride. She was Correggiesque, in that she was splendid and glowing, graceful, and yet a trifle out of drawing, much in the manner of Antonio Allegri Correggio's masterpieces. Even the most superficial observer could note the tenuous "out of drawing" aspect about her. Exquisitely pretty, virginal, yet queerly, somehow, not quite perfectly cast for the part; though she moved through the ceremony with clock-like precision.

After it was all over and she had attended to the last bit of polite gesticulation required of her, Miriam went to her car; climbed in before the chauffeur could jump out to open and close the door for her. Snapped out the one word, "Home!"

As soon as the car had drawn away, the set smile vanished from her face. She sat rigid, staring straight ahead. Emotion mounted in her until she grew afraid of the moment when the car should stop. So long as it speeded briskly its motion held in check the tension within her.

But her home was not far. Inevitably the car drew up into the driveway. Miriam did not move. The chauffeur got out and opened the door for her. Still she did not move; still she stared stonily in front of her; exquisite as a perfectly carved figurine, small, dainty; yet sharp and hard, with the poised brilliance of a neatly balanced slender spear.

She was seeing Elaine in white, looking like a soft angel. Elaine, so daintily colored and fragile; so golden and blue and creamy white. She suddenly remembered that Elaine and Hyde would soon enter Winton Hall together, the great new house which Hyde's father had had built for them, and the thought filled her with a cold, unreasoning fury. No physical indignity could have enraged her so completely as the thought of that couple in the great new house, *her* house! Mr. Winton, out of pure lethargy, had been only too delighted to place the construction of the huge showplace into Miriam's eager hands. Never before had she thrown herself into anything with such complete abandon. Every dream of richness and splendor she had ever had took shape in the form of mortar, brick, and stone. The stark magnificence of the marble floors, the austere majesty of the mahogany and teak-wood furniture, the imposing lushness of the velvet hangings;

all exhaled the very essence of Miriam Atwell's personality. Mr. Winton had permitted himself to be sworn to secrecy concerning her part in the project, since he admired her modesty, and was not at all averse to being credited with the brilliance and energy of Winton Hall's conception.

As each beam went into place, Miriam's mad desire to become mistress of the place herself deepened. She pictured it as the only fit setting for her own gem-like magnificence. She visualized great parties, with herself as the focal point surrounded by an orbit of talent, genius and inferior wealth. She *was* this house, and this house was she. The thought of Elaine and Hyde living in it, dulling its brilliance, pawing its fine antique pieces, maddened her infinitely worse than that of physical violation.

"Here we are, please, Miss."

Jerking out of her reverie she stared at the chauffeur as though she had never seen him before. Realized that he was handsome, clean, strong and youthful. Previously she had often noted this in an abstract way. Now she scrutinized him in new concentration. Had he, she thought, a better economic status he would be as desirable a male as Hyde; he was certainly as good-looking … nice manners … respectful … always had admired her, she knew, but had never presumed. At the moment she hated him. Seeing it in her eyes and feeling it in that way humans have of feeling strong emotions passing from one to another, he looked surprised.

Getting out of the car she went into the house. Her father had been dead for a great many years. Her mother had remained after the wedding ceremony and intended to have dinner with friends who lived near the church.

She walked up the stairs to her room. Stood in the center of the floor angrily. Surveyed the room. She had never paid any attention to its decorations. It was a typically feminine room.

Fluffy lace curtains. Dainty dressing table covered with typically feminine articles of the toilette. Fluffy, wispy lacey things in the closets. Row upon row of dainty shoes and slippers, all of reasonably good quality; but suddenly she was oppressed with an overwhelming sense of their bourgeois mediocrity. She thought of Elaine, blessed with surroundings of an exquisite magnificence which would be lost upon her while she was forced to exist in this atmosphere of second-rate excellence. A blinding rage engulfed her like a mad torrent of white-hot, molten steel.

She was hardly aware of getting into action.... Found herself yanking at the wispy curtains. They came down. Picking up a bottle from the dressing table she smashed it upon the floor. An overpowering scent of perfume filled the room. She stared down at herself, in the virginal costume of a bridesmaid. Tore the costume from her; ripped it to shreds in a violence of rage she had never known before.

The dainty lingerie beneath enraged her still more. It made her smooth flesh crawl when she became conscious of the shoddy feel of it. Ripping it off she threw it upon the floor; stood nude, white, vibrating with rage.... Glanced across the room into the dressing table mirror. Saw there a picture of perfect womanhood. Hard, firm, superbly shaped young breasts. Slim column of warmed marble torso. Narrow boyish hips and thighs. All of it rendered super-white by contrast with her smooth, shiny black hair.... Flashing brown eyes. Fascinated she approached nearer to the mirror in new awe. What she saw, she realized, was entrancing—yet she hated it. She would have liked to tear at it the way she had snatched at the curtains and rended her soft garments.... That supple, charming creature in the mirror ... she was the person who would give her dreams substance. She felt a bleak revulsion for the creamy flesh, yet she knew that its sensuous magnetism was the philosopher's stone that would draw Hyde to her.

Naked she threw herself upon the bed and writhed in anger and torment, trying to ward off and push away the things which sought to fill her mind. Elaine, soft and golden and blue and white, who would never need wealth or security for happiness, showered by blind stupid providence with ridiculous excesses of both while she herself was slipping into the bleak void.

She was conscious, as she forced herself to lie still upon the bed, of having been waiting all the years so far, for something to happen, never quite knowing what it was to be; but she had always had the feeling ... even back into those dim early days when father had been alive.

Through high school and college she had always half unconsciously been thinking: "Not this—not this—but something else—something which is to come later."

And then the glorious but bitterly brief plunge into the glittering pool of mature society. It was not personalities that fascinated Miriam, for she despised most people for themselves. No, it was the intrigue, the sense of wealth and power and cunning locked in bitter combat below the surface which overwhelmed her like an opiate. Now she had but one more desperate chance to live the only life that was worth living.

She couldn't stand it any more. Not given much to drinking she decided to have a highball.... Rang. Nobody came. Angrily she stepped to the intercommunicating house 'phone and dialed. The cook answered. The maid was out; she remembered now that she had been given the afternoon and evening off. There was no longer any butler.... Frozen assets had sent him away. Just the cook, the maid and Max, the chauffeur.

She paced the floor, feverish, tortured. There would have to be a way out somehow ... she couldn't stand any more of this. Not that floating vision of Elaine, like an angel, promising to *love,* honor and *obey*—! Obey? Why don't they include enjoy? Good God.

The rage welled up again. Without thought she went back to the telephone. Dialed the garage. Max answered. Now that he had answered she had no idea why she had called him. After a long pause she said:

"You know how to mix a highball, don't you?"

"Certainly, Miss."

"Well, go to the kitchen and get the stuff from the cook; the maid's out. Mix two and bring them up here."

"Did you say *two,* Miss?"

"Yes, I said two—and hurry up."

"Yes, Miss."

She resumed her pacing of the floor, thinking swiftly. The cook would wonder. To hell with her. Those days were past when one need fear servants; servants nowadays were in constant terror of losing their jobs. And if she reported the incident to her mother—what difference—she was twenty-five. Free, white and female!

Max, coming up with highballs. Why in Heaven's name had she asked him to do that she wondered.

Max, week after week, silent and respectful, but always, when he looked at her, concealing with smooth, well-trained perfection, his natural male sense of disturbance when he found himself in close contact with a superbly formed and strikingly pretty female. He was older than he looked, she knew. She remembered her mother telling her something about his having had a better education than the average chauffeur; he had been in some sort of business for himself once.

There was a knock on the door. For a moment she was panic stricken. Jumping up from the bed she hurried to an open closet and jerked out the first negligee her hand encountered. Wrapped it around her. Called out:

"Come in."

Max entered with two highballs upon a silver tray. His eyes went round with surprise when he saw the room, looked at the broken perfume bottle: smelled the intoxicating fragrance with which the room was heavy. Putting the tray quickly down he knelt to pick up fragments of the bottle. She watched him in a daze. His strong, well-knit figure was ludicrous, dedicated to the task of picking up small particles of glass. He was best displayed behind the wheel of a car, guiding it with effortless precision; looking, in his smart, gray uniform, like a viking at the prow of a brave little ship.

"Pardon, Miss, the highballs."

... Picked up the tray. Stood before her with it. She made no move to touch the glasses.... Boldly met his eyes. They were nice, hazel eyes. She became aware that she was all but shouting a challenge at him, and that he was comprehending, though there was no word spoken. She watched the parade of emotions across his eyes as he stared back at her. First had come surprise; then puzzlement, alarm, gladness, daring ... now it was she who was afraid.

He turned away from her. Put the tray down again upon a small table. Turned back to her. His strong arms went around her without his uttering a word. He drew her to him tightly. It was hard for her to breathe, so closely did his arms surround her and pull her against him.

But still she stared the challenge at him; and now he was completely heartened. He smiled at her in a way intended to be reassuring, so much as to say: "Never mind, Miss, I'm not a fool. I know you're not in love with me ... and I know my place ... I won't presume afterward."

She wanted to shout back to this unspoken statement of his: "You're all wrong, but—"

She did not resist as he picked her up and carried her across the room. She shut her eyes. His lips over her body caused her flesh to creep. She wanted to strike him; instead she kept her eyes closed.

Unconsciously, now, she tried to resist; but it was futile. Though stronger than the average young lady, she was a weakling in his arms.

Eyes still closed she ceased to resist. As matters progressed she was conscious only of pain, distress, impatience and disappointment. She had thought that this might change things; bring into her life some new element which would make the fact of Elaine's marriage of less consequence.

And then he was again the respectful servant. His eyes questioned her; but she stared back at him unresponsively.... Uttered two words:

"Get out."

Not, seemingly, at all surprised or disconcerted he left.

Disgusted and annoyed she picked up one of the highballs and drank it down.

Nothing, she mourned, had been changed; she had merely made a fool of herself and gained nothing by it.... Save that she did have an odd sense of having gotten even with somebody for something, which made matters a bit more bearable, though revenge was not pleasant when no one knew anything about it.

After a time she drank the other highball. Lay down upon the bed. Closed her eyes. At length a new thought brought surcease and even a sense of exuberance.

... Since her experiment had ended thus, in blankness, disappointment and annoyance, wouldn't Elaine's, perhaps, end in quite the same way? She felt that it would, and was aware of a growing conviction that she could keep Elaine from ever becoming a real wife to Hyde. And then Hyde and she ... the thought disgusted her, but the disgust faded quickly when she beheld herself as mistress of Winton Hall. Miriam sat up and was almost happy.

# CHAPTER SIX
## *MARRIAGE*
## *NIGHT NIGHTMARE*

T HE FROZEN ASSETS were capable even of holding part of the warmth of a honeymoon in abeyance.... And, anyway, Elaine and Hyde had done everything ... seen everything. Foreign travel would be no novelty to them; almost nothing could be novel except the one thing they were experimenting with: marriage. To go quietly home, after the wedding; give a housewarming for intimate friends, following the ceremony ... spend the first evening in their own home ... that would be an unusual experience.

It was a pretty-enough little place. French chateau effect. Stucco, with brown wood. Twenty-two rooms. A four-car garage. Several acres of their own ground; with a private driveway off the trunk road.

Hyde, alone in his bedroom, felt ill at ease. There was a certain feel about the room which made him uncomfortable. He couldn't have said precisely what it was. As to detail he could discover nothing wrong; but it was the kind of room he could never be comfortable in.

He thought longingly of his hideout on Manhattan. Be swell, he decided, to kidnap Elaine and take her there.... Or take her to his rooms at his own home, several miles away. Pacing the floor in his dressing gown he tried to assure himself that after he had lived in the room for a while he could so knock things around in it as to make it feel like the sort of room a man might inhabit.

Elaine had said she'd knock. He was tired; but not too tired. He abated his pacing sufficiently long to pour a spot of whiskey... : Tossed it off without a chaser. Glanced at the clock.... Nearly two o'clock in the morning.

Going to one of the windows he pushed it open. It was a bright, chill night. He filled his lungs with the cool night air. The moon was coldly, steely bright and sharply outlined the nearby trees in blue steel light. There was not a breath of breeze; everything was still and quiet, as though waiting with tense ominousness. He tried to imagine what Elaine could be doing.... Remembered the hectic night with Sally Tuttle. The memory stirred him so that he prickled all over. Sally was pretty and desirable ... but she was *déclassé*.... Elaine, in the next room; a thousand times as pretty; a million times as desirable, and *not déclassé*. Would he dare to—Closing the window he resumed his pacing; hoping that she might hear his footsteps and realize that she was taking an unconscionably long time to summon her husband.

In the next room Elaine, white and tense, came to the realization that there was nothing else that could be done to delay matters. Having bathed with meticulous attention to detail, she had powdered, perfumed and made herself up as though she were going to the premiere of a Eugene O'Neill play with Miriam.... With Miriam! The thought stirred her deeply. She would have given anything to have been back with Miriam again, instead of trembling on the verge of a step that terrified her. She recalled Miriam's account of the childhood incident in her bedroom with sickening clarity. Funny about that chauffeur of Miriam's ... that Max person. People talked.... Such a handsome young chauffeur ... in the employ of a pretty young lady who was known not to be interested in any of the men in her set. She'd remarked upon it once to Miriam. She could hear Miriam's contralto voice:

" 'Talking?' Let them talk. To hell with them. Suppose I *were* having an *affaire* with Max? What business should it be of anyone's but my own?"

She'd been convinced at the time that Miriam was telling the truth when she intimated that there was no basis for such gossip. Still....

Again she heard the steady pacing in the next room. Damn him, she said inwardly. Her hands were cold, and she was afraid ... desperately so. But this couldn't go on all night. She helped herself to another liberal drink; this time an entire small glass full of straight whiskey. As she swallowed it she realized that she had had more to drink, since the wedding ceremony that afternoon, than she had ever before imbibed during one day. It was odd, she thought, that she didn't feel the effects of it.... But when the last glassful hit bottom she did begin to feel dizzy.

When she rose from the bench in front of her dressing table her dizziness became acute. With the dizziness came a certain desperate courage. Swiftly crossing the room she opened the door which separated her own suite from her husband's. Stopping his pacing he turned toward her expectantly. Moving quickly through the door he took her into his arms.

... Felt, at once, the absence of anything beneath her negligee ... the soft, warm contours of her body; the freshness and virginal youth of her.

"I certainly kept you waiting a long time, didn't I?"

He glanced down at her. "It's all right, dear; perhaps you'd rather just go on to sleep. You must be tired out."

"... Oh, I'm not too tired."

His arm around her, they walked to the center of the room. She sank into a chair.

"Like a drink?" He was aware as he asked it of an unnatural stiffness in his manner. There was constraint of the unwieldiest sort between them.

"Don't mind," she replied.

He poured out a drink for each of them. She gulped hers down, and a moment later he saw a slightly glassy appearance come over her eyes.... Realized that she had been drinking heavily.... So, he reflected inwardly, she was still afraid ... reluctant. Far from feeling disappointment at this realization of her feelings he was elated. Thus *should* a gentlewoman comport herself under such circumstances. He was tired of the too willing ones.

"Perhaps you'd better lie down, Elaine."

Rising a trifle unsteadily she went over to the bed; sat down upon it. He pushed her gently back until she lay across it, feet touching the floor, body reclining. Her hair was down. It was rather long. It spilled like liquid gold over the orchid silk counterpane. He sat down beside her. Her eyes were staring up at him, filled with fear. He was delighted to know that she felt afraid, reluctant. It was like capture and force ... something distinctly thrilling about it ... something age old.... So vastly different from the usual attitude of the women he had known.

"... Want another drink?"

She nodded.

Rising he procured just one drink, not now feeling the necessity for any additional stimulation on his own part. She sat up and drank; then lay down again.... Watching him silently. After a pause he reached down and gently disarranged her negligee. He saw a rush of color suffuse her face and neck; as he watched, the color spread down to her bosom. Enveloped her lovely, ivory breasts in a warmth of pink. His scalp prickled. She stirred uneasily. Closed her eyes…. The natural reluctance of a gentlewoman, he surmised exultantly.

"Do you mind?"

She merely shook her head in answer to his question. He became bolder.

One hand crept softly down along sheer silky warm loveliness. Stirring again uneasily she threw a shapely arm across her eyes. Now she was all revealed. Hers was the anatomy of a nymph. He gazed with an arresting awe. To look for a time and not to touch was a sort of negative ecstasy which he indulged for several minutes. He marveled that she could have come to marry him at all.

"Like another drink?"

She thickly murmured acquiescence.

He rose and got it. Lifted her up to drink it. She was plainly drunk now. Dazed. As though hypnotized. He threw away restraint.

She mumbled unintelligibly. He smiled to himself with delight. All around them there was quiet; locked away from the world, they were … in a room that held the perfume of fragrant young womanhood. The lamp before the dressing table was on, and another near the door. Rising he turned on all the other fixtures so that the room blazed with light…. Shook her. She mumbled thickly and turned over. It occurred to him that she was in that state of drunkenness which would make it very unlikely that she would, in the morning, recall anything that had passed between them.

After a long time the 'phone in his suite rang shrilly. It was the one 'phone in the house still connected; the others, including Elaine's private 'phone, having been disconnected for the night.

Weakly he went in to answer it.

"This is Hyde—who is it?" He was conscious of speaking with extreme petulance.

"It's Miriam."

" 'Miriam?' " he repeated dazedly. He noted that she was extremely excited.

"Yes, it's Miriam, *Miriam*—may I speak to Elaine?"

" 'Elaine?' "

"Yes, for God's sake, don't you know the woman? You married her this afternoon."

"Yes, I know," he repeated, groggy and confused.

"Well, may I speak to her?"

"She's asleep, Miriam."

"Well, can't you wake her up?"

He hesitated. He knew Miriam quite well; remembered that she was Elaine's closest friend.

"No, I don't think I can wake her up, Miriam, she's; she's—"

"Well ...?" Miriam prompted brusquely after a long wait.

"She's out."

" 'Out—!' What do you mean?"

"Passed out."

"Elaine *passed out*!—she never drank that much before."

"No, I guess not."

"You sure you can't wake her up?"

"Positive."

"Do you mind if I come over?"

"*Now!* Why! It's nearly three o'clock."

"Do you *mind?*"

"Why, no, I guess not; but what's wrong, what on earth do you want to come over here this time of morning for?"

"If Elaine's passed out she'll be sick as a dog in the morning."

"That's right," Hyde conceded, distinctly worried. "Yes, that's right. Maybe you better come at that." He tried desperately to collect his thoughts, continued:

"I'll go downstairs and wait for you. I'll put you in one of the guest rooms."

"Never mind that; I'll sleep with Elaine."

"With Elaine!"

"... Well, do you *mind?*"

"No, I don't mind, only ..."

"I'll be right over." She hung up the receiver. Puzzled, confused and weak, Hyde went back into Elaine's room, in the throes of a sudden panic of embarrassment. Things were in devilish shape. What in hell, he wondered, would he do? Miriam lived only a short distance away. She'd arrive shortly. He cursed her for an erratic fool of a woman, and then was glad of her coming too ... things might be damned awkward and embarrassing in the morning. Devil of a mess.... He had been more drunk, himself, than he had realized, he now was aware.

He felt trapped.... Listened for the sound of Miriam's car coming down the private drive.... What a mess for Miriam to see.

He paced the floor, confused and embarrassed. If he could get Elaine into another room ... he shook her; but she was past all rousing. Breathing heavily, obviously in the deepest stages of drunkenness. What a mess, he groaned. He tried to pick her up and carry her out of the room, but it was impossible ... all of his strength had temporarily fled.

He heard a car come down the driveway. Fear took him; yet he was glad too. Hastily he threw Elaine's torn negligee over her and went below stairs. Opened the door. Miriam hurried into the lower hallway.

"Where is she?"

"Upstairs."

Miriam went toward the stairs. Hyde went up beside her, managing with difficulty to keep up with her.

"You can think I'm crazy if you like," Miriam spat out at him, "but I couldn't sleep. I had the feeling that Elaine needed me—that something terrible was happening to her. We've been close friends for years … you feel that way about your friends."

"Yes," Hyde mumbled, trembling, as they opened the door that led into Elaine's suite. The lights were still all blazing.

Quickly crossing the floor he entered his own suite. Shut the door. Again paced the floor, thoroughly sober now, his nerves jangling.

With the full realization that he had been to all intents and purposes out of his head for at least an hour, came the inner conviction that passion was indeed a devastating drug … habit forming. The habit, he explained to himself—as though he were counseling another—subtly changed one's character until one day the new being crawled out and took complete possession.

His door was opened. Miriam stood upon the threshold, eyes bright.… Holding Elaine's favorite riding crop which she had taken from the wall of Elaine's room. She moved slowly and determinedly toward him. He backed away.

# CHAPTER SEVEN
## *MIRIAM'S WHIP*

HYDE OPENED his eyes. He was conscious of pain. It was as though he were wrapped in heavy, hot cords, covered with tinsel that sawed into his flesh every time he moved.

Gingerly he reached up and felt his face. Luckily there were no contusions there; but there was a painful swelling on the back of his head. That had been, he supposed, what put him out.

No doubt she'd finally hit him with something heavy and knocked him into complete unconsciousness; then thrown him upon the bed.

He was in his pyjamas and bathrobe. Lying still, he listened intently. The door between his suite and Elaine's was closed.

Wonderingly he traced back down the lanes of his memory.... Miriam coming at him with that riding crop.... Then bringing it down across his right shoulder.... A torrent of blows, seeming to last through an eternity; then finally the terrific blow which had stunned him.

He wondered if the servants had heard; if a doctor had been called ... if a desperate scandal were brewing. Groaning he closed his eyes. But he could not flee back into unconsciousness. His head ached intolerably and his whole body was aflame with pain.

Surprise glowed in him. Mounted to a flame of interest which took his mind a little from his terrific sense of unease. Miriam. How thoroughly different from what he had supposed her to be.... How completely he had misjudged her. He'd always thought of her before as one of those possessed of what he identified as the "Greenwich Village Grimace."

... One saw individuals all over New York and vicinity ... with the Greenwich Village Grimace. Neurotic, frustrated, starved souls in half-starved bodies.... On the edge of the arts.... Far removed from the upper reaches of social life.... Existing in a limbo, with only a Grimace to shield them from the contempt of others ... with only a Grimace to be used in attack against everyone who to any degree succeeded, financially, socially, or artistically.

... See them on the streets, in the subways; at theatres, everywhere.... Viewing everyone as "types." Acting vastly superior; while established writers and artists of standing were perfectly natural, without pose, and good company anywhere.

Miriam was not quite "in" so far as Long Island social life was concerned. Her mother and she were not so well off as most of those in the set within which they circulated. But how vastly different she was. And pretty. God how pretty. Her eyes bright with hate for him. Her lithe body swinging the crop with amazing vigor. Her strikingly white skin, and her jet hair and dark brown eyes—! No, she was not the type he had supposed. Not the Grimace type. The Grimace type never *did* anything forthright, like striking persons with something solid ... they struck with epigrams; or let go Parthian sneers ... or damned with a drawled: "My, what an interesting *type*...." As though the whole human race, outside themselves, were merely specimens to be observed with faint amusement.

He heard the door between his suite and his wife's move slowly, cautiously. Opening his eyes he watched with apprehension. Miriam's head became visible. Her eyes were bright and large. She peered in at him. Seeing that he was awake she came in and closed the door softly. He stared at her, half in fright, half in awe as she made her way toward the bed. She was in one of Elaine's black nightgowns. Her exquisite shoulders were bare except for the gown's shoulder loops. He had never seen such perfect shoulders, such vivid warm whiteness.

As she passed between him and the window he saw her bodily outlines clearly revealed. He drew in his breath, involuntarily. Such slimness and perfection of line. And there was strength in her; she would, and could fight. She came over and sat down upon the bed. He stared up at her without speaking. It came to him that, oddly enough, she was frightened too. He tried to think what it could be that frightened her; perhaps, he thought, she had supposed him to be dead. He was conscious, too, a trifle shamedly, that he desired this woman.

… Those years of sensual living … were bearing fruit. He had always supposed he could "take it or leave it" so far as such things went … but now!

"Well …?" Miriam questioned, in her low contralto. She feared that Elaine might have been just sober enough to let something slip about their talk before the wedding. Had that been the case, Hyde might have been clever enough to sense what she was up to. He saw that for some strange reason she was bluffing, that she was fearful of him.

"How's Elaine?" he asked.

"Pretty bad. She woke up and I had the servants bring her some breakfast. She'll have to stay in bed all day. She's asleep again, now; I sent out for some sleeping tablets."

"Yes, yes, I know," he interrupted. "I'm sorry, Miriam."

He lay silent, and she stared down at him as though awaiting attack. He tried to imagine what it could be that she feared. She acted as though she expected to be accused; denounced on some count. He had supposed that *he* would be the one on the defensive; obviously it was she. Racking his brains for a reason to account for it he could find none. Said:

"Did the servants—"

"No, they didn't hear. This morning I merely explained that both of you'd had a bit too much to drink last night and that Elaine had sent for me to take care of her early this morning. They swallowed it."

"What did Elaine say?"

"Nothing."

"Is she going to leave me?"

Miriam knit her brows and did not reply.

"I can't blame you, Miriam, for what you did last night. And, by God, you certainly did it thoroughly. I'm sore as a boil all over."

She received this information coldly. Suggested:

"Take a warm bath and then rub down with cold cream or something greasy like that—"

"Would you mind telling me what you cracked me over the head with?"

Carelessly she informed:

"The butt end of the crop."

"You are a lady of action, aren't you?"

"What are you going to do about it, Hyde?"

"About what?"

"Everything."

She was watching him narrowly, and still afraid; he wondered again what on earth it could be that she feared.

"I don't know what you mean, Miriam."

"Are you going to tell anybody about—"

"Good Lord, no. Are you?"

"I'll keep my mouth shut if you will."

His eyes on her face, which now held an inscrutable expression, he pondered deeply; but his aching head evolved no solution to the mystery of *her* being afraid of people knowing about last night's happenings. If anyone were to be fearful of details getting around he ought to be the one.

"That's good of you, Miriam.... I mean, to keep it to yourself."

She appeared, he noted, greatly relieved; evidently his reply had for some strange reason reassured her.

"I think I'd better stay with Elaine, don't you, Hyde, until she's feeling better?" Here was the foothold! she thought triumphantly. Nothing could dislodge her from this house now.

"Yes, by all means stay."

"I'd better stay all night tonight, perhaps?"

"Yes, indeed, stay all night. If people call today *you* see them. Tell them we both got cockeyed drunk."

"All right, I'll do that."

She was about to go. Reaching out painfully he detained her by putting a hand on her smooth, warm forearm. He felt her muscles tauten under his grasp as though she were getting ready to throw off his hand and strike him. Her hatred, her obvious resistance, was obliquely enticing. He became confidential:

"Look here, Miriam; I owe you some explanation further than the one I gave you. It's hard to say.... To phrase intelligently.... You see; none of us, in our set, have been ... well, you know what I mean. Elaine, for some reason, evidently kept herself aloof from that sort of thing."

"Evidently," she agreed. He winced at the obvious meaning of this, remembering the state of the room last night.

"You think I'm pretty low, don't you, Miriam?"

"Yes." She said it with great decision; then cautiously modified it to: "But, after all, who am I to judge?"

"You're right, I am pretty low. I'll lay off the liquor from now on and it probably won't happen again."

" 'Probably?' "

He frowned, only now aware of his slip.

"I don't think you need to worry about its happening again while I'm around, Hyde; and I expect to be here quite a lot.... And the riding crop's still in there.... And if you should be so indiscreet as to make a fuss about matters don't forget that I could tell a pretty ugly story about what happened here last night. If Elaine's father should know..."

"She'll probably tell him."

"Not if I advise her otherwise."

"She'll no doubt leave me."

"Well ... it would hardly be wise for that to happen so soon ... there'd be all sorts of rumors and ..."

She was bluffing. He was sure of it. He wished he could think why and on behalf of what; but his throbbing head was not now a ready instrument for ratiocination.... And, besides, he was not overmuch worried. Let her stay. There was something in the notion which did not displease him.... That ivory, pliant warm body around the house wasn't a half bad idea. Inwardly he cursed himself for having such notions; but realized, even as he did so, that the matter was entirely out of his hands.

Throwing off his restraining hand she rose. Walked slowly, gracefully, toward the door. Went through it and closed it gently after her. A moment later he heard the key turn in the lock.

Elaine looked very small and childlike asleep in the large bed. With great difficulty Miriam had remade the bed with materials from the linen closet in the hall. Sitting on the bed she stroked the sleeping girl's forehead. Elaine stirred in her drugged sleep, as though having an unpleasant dream.

Miriam had entered the house that morning with only the vaguest of impressions that an opportunity existed, and that it was ripe. Now fortune had furnished her with not only the tools with which to destroy the marriage, but with a means of gaining a formidable hold over Hyde himself. His blundering confession had assured her that he had no knowledge of her insidious campaign to keep Elaine from him and, perhaps even more important, it had informed her of the strange, unnatural desires that possessed him. The thought disgusted her, but she smiled smugly knowing that she would know how to hold him when the divorce came. She was strangely grateful that her efforts to win Hyde away from Elaine before the wedding had failed. Broken engagements are too easily mended, but a marriage shattered as this one was being shattered was hopelessly beyond repair.

She would have to be patient and clever, she reasoned. She had no hold on Hyde as yet, and if he discovered what she was about, he might easily turn her out of the house and succeed in winning Elaine back. She must keep Elaine remote, disillusioned until he was driven elsewhere to satisfy his physical drives. And then, she would be waiting. Hating him, loathing him, she would submit.

# CHAPTER EIGHT
## *TWO IN A TUB*

T HE FOLLOWING day Elaine felt better. After breakfast Miriam returned from a drive home to find her sitting up reading.

"Where's Hyde?" Elaine asked.

"Don't know," Miriam told her a trifle crossly. "He didn't stay here last night; probably went into town and stopped at some hotel." Miriam turned away and busied herself with unnecessarily straightening things around the room.

For a long time neither one spoke. Elaine had put down her book. Finally Miriam asked:

"How do you feel?"

"All right. It was good of you to come when I needed someone."

Miriam went over and sat down on the edge of the bed.

"Are you going to tell your father ... anyone ...?"

"About Hyde—about—?"

Miriam nodded.

"No, why should I?"

Miriam shrugged.

"You must see that you're not going to be able to make a go of this marriage business."

Elaine did not reply. Miriam went on, not meeting the other's eyes, but gazing off out the window:

"Why not go away? ... Europe.... Anywhere."

"So soon? It would appear very strange to everyone, if Hyde didn't go too."

"Well, what *are* you going to do?"

Elaine stirred uneasily.

"You must see that you can't go on with him."

"I've an idea, Miriam, that he'll be easy enough to handle from now on. I'll bet he's ashamed of himself. It's strange he should have acted that way. He didn't seem to be at all that sort."

"And you're going to remain here ... stay married to him—permit him the freedom of your bedroom?"

"No. Not the latter.... But if he's that sort he'll probably have interests elsewhere, don't you think? He won't be likely to bother me when he finds I don't want him to—and I've certainly got an excellent excuse to refuse now.

"Yes," Miriam agreed, "perhaps that's best.... And since he has interests elsewhere...."

Elaine marked the place in her book. Sighed.

"I thought it all might eventuate quite differently; but life seems to be rotten and dull ... what is there?"

"You don't remember what happened the other night, do you?"

Elaine's eyes widened. "No, why do you ask?"

"I was looking for a book to read in the library yesterday, and found one in Hyde's own private cabinet. I found these inside, but can't decide whether to show them to you or not." Miriam produced a set of pornographic photographs she had obtained from Rene Mersault, a lecherous little French novelist of her acquaintance. He had been rather startled by the request, but had acquiesced readily in hopes of creating a favorable atmosphere for certain future plans he had concerning her.

"They are not the sort of thing that I would ordinarily show to any human being, but they will undoubtedly help you to understand what sort of an animal you are married to."

Elaine evinced a surprising curiosity. "Let me see them."

She paled at the first one, and alternately flushed red and white as she went through the pile. They seemed to have a hypnotic effect on her. She was plainly revolted, and yet fascinated. Miriam noted that she went through them a second time with an intensifying mixture of interest and disgust.

At last Miriam advised, "You'd better give them back to me, I'll have to put them back before he discovers them gone."

Elaine got up. She was a trifle unsteady.

"Head still aches ... dizzy ..." she explained, when it was necessary for Miriam to put an arm around her to support her. "A warm bath might...."

"I'll help you," Miriam said firmly.

Miriam led her toward the bathroom. There was a square, green-tiled pool, sunk into the floor; a shower above it. Miriam turned on both the taps, and set a thermometer to floating in the water on its black rubber, air-inflated base.

Elaine sat down on a glass chair near the tub and watched.

Miriam took up a large jar of bath salts and sprinkled them liberally around the pool. Kneeling, she put a slender white hand into the water. Elaine watched the hand. Against the background of green tile it was a remarkably white and daintily impressive hand. The pool was filling fast with scented water. Miriam frequently glanced at the thermometer, and tested the water with her hand; increasing or diminishing the hot and cold water by turns.

At last she turned off both taps. Gave the water a final test.

"I might as well get in with you," she suggested. "... Help you best that way, perhaps."

Elaine did not reply.

Without looking toward her, Miriam disrobed. Elaine watched as the other's supple, white body was revealed. At last, wholly nude, Miriam turned toward her and met her eyes.

"Want me to help you take off—"

As though suddenly reminded of something Elaine slipped out of her bed pyjamas, her pink-white body matching in superb contours the whiter body of the other. Elaine sat down on the edge of the pool; dangled her legs in the water and slid into its perfumed depths. Submerged in the soothing, healing warmth to her throat. Miriam slid in beside her, also submerged.

"This feels good," Elaine said, touched by the strange exuberance which usually comes to humans when they are partly submerged in comfortably warm water. The warmth and perfume brought a pleasant tingle of sensuousness to her. She shut her eyes.

Unpleasant as the experience with Hyde had been, it had awakened her in some way.... Brought alive a latency in her which had been long dormant.

"Stand up and I'll soap you," Miriam directed.

Trembling a trifle Elaine stood up, submerged now only to a short way above her knees. Miriam rubbed a huge sponge with soap; kneaded it into lather; applied it to the satin smooth pink-warmed skin of the other. Presently Elaine was all but hidden in lather. Miriam put down the sponge and worked with her hands, smoothing the lather over the lithe young body of the other.

"Now sit down on the edge," Miriam instructed. Elaine sat down on the edge of the pool.

"Give me your legs, one at a time."

Elaine raised one of her legs. Alternately Miriam lathered them. Then Elaine lathered her all over. When she had rinsed, Miriam climbed out of the water and investigated the cabinet above the pool. There were several bathing caps there. Selecting two of them she handed one to Elaine and put on the other.

They stepped under the shower, after Miriam had graduated it to a warmth approximately that of the water in the tub.

Needles of warm water pricked tender skin, sent the blood to tingling everywhere. They stood very close together under the shower, so that both might be completely included in it.

Miriam reached out and slightly turned the black porcelain graduating handle which changed the mixture of shower water. The shower became gradually colder. Again she increased the chill of the water. Elaine uttered a sharp exclamation as the water became increasingly colder. When it was thoroughly chilly they clung together, for warmth, under the assault of needle-like streams of cold water.

Finally Miriam shut off the shower and they climbed out of the pool. Taking up one of the huge towels which lay piled on a shelf in one corner of the room, Miriam rubbed down the other briskly, until she was a glowing, pink, perfumed nymph.

Elaine, feeling much better now, rubbed Miriam down with one of the towels.

They scampered into the other room. Lighted cigarettes. Lay down together upon the bed.

It was long after midnight when Hyde returned, feeling much better after a long sleep in his hideout, away from the scene of his misbehavior. His return, he assured himself, was for the purpose of apologizing deeply and humbly for his appalling behavior; though privately in one of the deeper recesses of his mind he felt no real great need for apology.... Resented the necessity for one.

He recalled with aversion a conversation he'd had with the young lady in charge of a book store near his hideout. One of those most superior and very coldly pretty women one saw increasingly more of, of late. They had discussed a sex novel he was minded to purchase. The young lady expressed a dislike for the book, basing her objections upon the fact that in it the characters were "too conscious" of what they were doing when they went through sexual exercises.

Her viewpoint, he knew, was a currently popular one among self-conscious members of the intelligentsia.... As if there were some virtue inherent in people not being conscious of what they did when they did it. He snorted in the dark, at the wheel of the car. It was a new religion growing up among the "cognoscenti," a new religion with circumscribing tenets and pious taboos.

... As though when Grecian maids met Grecian warriors returned from battle aching for female company, and were tumbled forthwith upon the greensward, the whole thing would be all right provided that neither the warriors nor the maidens were conscious of what they were doing. What rot!

Turning off the trunk road into his own private driveway he slowed down.

As he approached, it occurred to him that there was an ominous quality to the house. It was a symbol to him now of the strange and macabre character change that had come over him with his marriage. He had thought by marriage to turn aside from the grossly obvious fleshly pleasures and find a form of passionate expression more substantial. Instead, he was aware, a dreadful psychological trick of some sort had been played upon him by nature, so that he had turned from a jovial beast into an intent, lecherous ogre of whom he was himself afraid, and before whom he stood, when he thought of it objectively, distressed and appalled and fearful ... wondering with some latent, childlike section of his mind, how to get back to a mental state more creditable than his present one.

The house was tenuously outlined by the moon at its back. Around it the tall, neatly trimmed trees stood like ghosts warning wayfarers that this was an odd and eerie house where it would be best that no innocent one tarry for fear of being bewitched by its influence. With sudden surprising clearness a passage he had never forgotten, from Poe, repeated itself in his mind:

"During the whole of a dull, dark, and soundless day in the autumn of the year, when the clouds hung oppressively low in the heavens, I had been passing alone, on horseback, through a singularly dreary tract of country; and at length found myself, as the shades of the evening drew on, within view of the melancholy House of Usher."

There was a light burning downstairs. As Hyde put his car in the garage he realized that the light was coming from the direction of the library.... And he also was aware of the real reason why he had returned. His blood leapt, with that almost insane craving that had strangely come to him. *Miriam!* That would be she in the library.

# CHAPTER NINE
## THE DEVIL, THE FLASH ...
## AND MIRIAM

M IRIAM GLANCED up from her book as Hyde entered.

"How's Elaine?" he inquired.

"Better."

He sat down near her.

"What'd she say?"

"Hadn't you better talk to her yourself?"

"Yes, I guess that's right."

"She's asleep now. Be all right by tomorrow."

"It was good of you to stay and take care of her."

"Don't mention it, Hyde."

He studied her, puzzled. She gave every evidence of being in a pleasanter state of mind toward him than she had been when he'd seen her last; yet he could have sworn, though he had no objective evidence upon which to base the assumption, that she was inwardly just as angry with him. After a moment she said:

"How do *you* feel?"

"Oh, I'm O. K. Kind of stiff and sore yet; but nothing to worry about."

"I'm sorry I was so precipitate, Hyde."

At her tone he scrutinized her closely; her eyes now were unfathomable.... And he was thinking of that slim, agile white soft body beneath the pyjamas she was wearing and the black silk gown over them.

"Are you going to stay here tonight, Miriam?"

She eyed him a trifle uncertainly.

"Yes."

Taking out his cigarette case he selected a cigarette and lit it; she already had a lighted cigarette near her on the edge of an ash tray.

"I suppose you don't think much of me, Miriam."

"I probably don't condemn you any more strongly than you do yourself."

"It's good of you to put it that way."

He paused for her to give some sign; but she remained enigmatical.

"If you knew me better than you do, Miriam, you might like me even less."

Again he waited, but there was no response. She sat as though carved from ivory; slim and white and inscrutable. The room was very still. Not a breath of air stirred in it. The smoke from their cigarettes went unwaveringly upward toward the high ceiling. The room was paneled as to both walls and ceiling in oak. There was a long oak table in the center of the floor. The walls, half way up, except for the window spaces, were lined with bookshelves. On the shelves were rows of books; the sort of books that everyone ought to read and nobody did anymore. He glanced toward the book she had laid face downward upon the table, open where she had been reading when he came in. The title was: "The Mad Nymph." The volume had a scarlet cover that was markedly incongruous in the conventional library with its rows of stern leather bindings: Hazlitt; Gibbon; Hawthorne; Longfellow; De Quincey.... And the book was also strangely out of consonance with Miriam. What sort was she really, he speculated. He had so woefully misjudged her twice; and now she appeared to be in an entirely different mood from any he had observed in her before. Her negligee was of a flimsy consistency. She sat with her limbs straight out before her, tiny feet firmly upon the floor. The negligee had settled in between her limbs, outlining the seductive proportions of her compact body.

The windows of the library were of small-paned, leaded glass; upon the floor there was a thick, dark brown rug. In one corner stood the only bit of bright coloration in the room, aside from the bright book which Miriam had brought in with her: a rather large spherical "world," which swung upon an axis; with all the different countries of the globe painted upon it in various colors.

A droll and rather silly thought came to him: The World, over there in the corner; the Flesh ... Miriam ... the Devil ... himself. A complete universe within the room. And such a monkish dignified room.... The World there in the corner; Miriam, whitely, superbly nude, a poem in flesh ... in this room ... the Devil.... Shaking himself out of his mad reverie, he forced himself to throw words against the maddening silence and the strange hypnotic effect it was having upon him as he stared abstractedly at the large many-colored globe in the corner:

"... You know how it is with music, Miriam." He was startled at his own words. Though he wasn't watching her, was still staring at the World in the corner, he felt her eyes center upon his face. Was he, he wondered, going crazy? It had sounded as though he were. He must manage to go on.... Make sense of what he had started to say. He wished to lift up his cigarette and put it into his mouth; draw deeply upon it, fill his lungs with the narcotic tobacco; but he dared not move until he had managed to make sense of his words; since, if he moved, he might make some gesture as inane as his words had been.

"You know how it is with music, Miriam." Again he stuck. There was a deathly stillness over everything.

He imagined that he heard a clock ticking nearby; but it couldn't be, he realized, the real ticking of a real clock. The ticks were much too fast ... frantically fast. The strong oak paneling ... dark ... her vivid white body against that background.

"The most exquisite music in the world," he went on, "played perfectly, but with the time doubled, and perhaps doubled again, would be nothing but cacophony." He knew that she was watching him and listening intently now; was aware that all along the lower depths of his mind had held that thought; that in some way his conscious mind had inhibited it from coming out. What was to follow, he speculated. There was more to it, back in his subconscious. He waited upon his own next words with as much, and, he was inclined to think, probably more impatience than she did. In his subconsciousness was a vast plan, all worked out as to detail ... of that he was sure now. His conscious mind was unfolding it a little at a time. He was aware of things subconsciously that he didn't know consciously ... and his inner self was working toward an objective, using this awareness and a fundamental instinctive urge of its own, sealed up within him, as impetus.

"It's much the same, Miriam, with life here in New York in this day and age. It's smoothly perfect, life, now, for most of us ... perfect in a superficial, dangerous way. But it's so fast nobody can make head or tail of it and it's all cacophony. Do you see what I mean? You are whirled along by the meaninglessness of it, not heeding the leitmotif because it's all cacophony, until one day the leitmotif, through unconscious repetition, becomes clear to you; and then it's too late, the motif goes on singing itself in you, like a song you find in your head when you wake up in the morning, and there's no way to get rid of it. Do you see what I mean?"

"Yes."

Her voice sounded cold and hard; but when he glanced covertly at her she smiled at him friendlily. He felt his inner self move on toward its goal; a goal about which he wondered as much as he had wondered what his inner self would produce to back up the mad opening sentence he had blurted out. Now that he came to think of it consciously, what his inner self had produced was pretty clever; what next might be evolving, he wondered. He felt strangely excited and elated.

"You see, Miriam, the leitmotif was in me, all jangled up in the heedless speed of the life I'd been leading; when I tried to change the record ... when Elaine and I—"

"I understand, *perfectly*, Hyde. Perfectly—far more than you realize—something like that happened to me too, and—"

She broke off with, he thought, no little agitation.

His inner self moved on:

"No, you don't see yet, Miriam. Not quite.... Not about me, at any rate. I suppose you're more or less persuaded that I *really* felt contrition.... That I was thinking of contrition just now, when I was silent and contemplative. It isn't true. I ... was thinking ... what a superb spectacle you'd make in this room, nude, against the richness of this oak paneling ... an element light and soft, midst all this heaviness. Something strong but agile, in all this ponderousness. I guess the leitmotif that sings itself in me is no new one. I suppose it's the same leitmotif you hear in most Oriental music—only with the Orientals it was all slow and its tempo perfect, exquisitely gauged to the movements of humans executing love gestures." He was amazed at his own dexterity and effrontery. She'd go get the crop now, he thought.

"In short, Miriam," he went on relentlessly, "married so short a time I find myself desiring you. So you see, you *didn't* comprehend. I am worse than you supposed."

"Have those windows shades?" she asked, amazing him and jarring him out of all subtlety, conscious or unconscious.

"Yes, I suppose so."

"Perhaps you'd better attend to them."

He gazed at her with an emotion approaching stupefaction, then rose and pulled down all the shades. Rising, she moved calmly to the door. Closed and locked it.... Then coolly and calmly stood revealed. He stared trembling. Too impressed to stop to wonder what had prompted her to such a thing.

... Slowly, spellbound, he went toward her. He had supposed that she would back away from him; but she did not. She stood still as the ivory statue she resembled. He stopped before her. Gazed down into her eyes. But he could discover nothing there.... What he felt—and knew to be true—came to him from her, he was sure, through some strange sort of apperception, rather than through any outward sign of hers. He knew that she did not want him, and yet was willing. Why this should be he did not stop to ponder.

He put his arms around her, and was a trifle surprised to find her hot to the touch. She had given such an impression of coldness that he had half expected to find her negatively cold, as ivory is negatively cold.

Afterward, when she had left the room and gone upstairs, he stood weakly in the center of the floor.

"Why? Why? Why?" his surface mind asked him over and over again; and his inner self smirked complacently, knowing something he could not fathom.

In the cursed house, he nervously assured himself, there was a mystery. The place was inescapably sinister. It gave him the creeps. There was almost anything in the air. Murder, even. When she had struck at him with the crop there had been the lust to kill in her eyes. Had it been a heavier weapon she would, he was persuaded, have murdered him.

And just now, when she had left the room—none of her dignity or coldness gone despite everything—there had been an emotion of the same sort emanating from her; as though, despite the fact that she had brought him exquisite joys she would still like to, and quite conceivably might, slay him.

He was tempted to flee back to his hideout; the one place left where he felt safe and comfortable. The cursed place, he raved inwardly, would drive him mad. Servants who crept around always out of sight. Trees that stood like sentinels, posted at regular intervals—by some damned landscape gardener who felt that nature was best propitiated in geometrical patterns. He could feel the trees outside the house standing guard duty now. They were unreasonable trees. They never appeared to stir or dance as did most trees. And the front of the house appeared to have a personification. A face. A deceitful, malicious face ... and that confounded room of his upstairs, furnished for a man by a man ... by a man who wasn't a man. A hell of a place for a man, who was a man, to sleep in. He moved—out of some queer conviction that he was forming a cabalistic and potent design by standing half way in between the globe in the corner and the red book on the table. This would never do, he told himself earnestly. Too much liquor ... too little to do ... too much drain on his nervous system through frantic excesses.

And there *was* some reason he hadn't fathomed yet why she had acted as she had. If he knew that reason—what a whip hand it would give him over her. She ... a gentlewoman. A rare bit. Not like the Sally Tuttles. If, he realized, he could discover what prompted such unusual behavior in her he could force her to submit not only to what she had undergone tonight, which was pleasant enough, but to all of the other delights of dalliance. She, who had beaten him with a crop, could be made to humble herself in the widest compliances that a potentate of Bagdad might demand of his abject slave girls. The blood beat at his temples; there was a motive behind it all, he assured himself. No doubt about that. He must stop running around in frantic circles and figure it out; ferret it out through captiousness, if necessary. Know it he must.

The first and obvious conjecture was, that she was secretly in love with him and, for some reason, too proud or too hurt by his ignoring her previously, and by his marriage, to let him know the truth. Yet now he was satisfied that that was not the explanation of her queer conduct, plausible though it appeared to be.

He mounted the stairs slowly, to disrobe and go to sleep in his uncomfortable suite. He would, he was aware, have much to occupy his mind.

As he climbed into bed he sighed heavily:

So *this*, he mourned bitterly, was the marriage which was to have been such a splendid new thing in his and Elaine's life.

He felt unhappy, disappointed and afraid.... But determined, nevertheless, to discover what mystery was at the bottom of it all.

# CHAPTER TEN
## *NOT PREPARED FOR*
## *MARRIAGE*

S O SHE WAS a wife, Elaine reflected.... And all she felt was a lethargy, a physical and mental weakness that would not be thrown off. Never, so far back as she could recall, had she spent so much time in bed.

It was ten and she still lay in bed. It was one of those first mild days, signaling the approaching termination of winter.

Her French windows were open wide. From where she lay in bed she could get a glimpse of the ocean, far off, sparkling in little patches through the trees. The sunshine and the fresh warm wind came into the window and moved small, light things around the room. There was that about the tone of the wind and the quality of the sunshine which stirred a vaguely adumbrated nostalgia in her.

She thought back to times in her youth when her father and mother had been very different kinds of people, and her grandmother had been alive.

Her grandmother had been a real type. With a fichu of lace at her throat, an old lady, she was one who was not in the least dismayed by the coming of old age.... An old lady who was glad enough to sit in corners with a shawl around her shoulders and smile kindly in her long silences, while others talked. So warm and cosy it had been near grandmother.... always full of sto-ries ... always full of placid explanations to charm away the fears of a child.

Dear old person of an age wiped out. Dad was always talking about what was wrong with the age.... What was really wrong with it, Elaine reflected whimsically, was that there were no more authentic grandmothers.

Her father, too, had been jollier in those days; and her mother. Now they were ever tense ... always acting as though they awaited a crisis.

When she had been small she had thought in terms of infi-nite areas of brightnesses. Somehow her grandmother's tales and her mother's and father's assurances had lighted up all the dark corners of the world, so that Sin, Sickness and Death became the fables, and Little Boy Blue and Cinderella were the realities.

Yes, they had protected her; sheltered her—watched over her—lied to her, with all good intentions. Done such a good job of this lying that even years of living had not quite disabused her mind of the thought of a world lit with brightnesses that over-shadowed all of the unpleasant things. She knew now for what it was she had been, in some puzzlement and confusion, waiting during those years of transition, in between adolescence and the present time.... Knew why it was that she had led a curiously uneventful life. She had been waiting to discover the world full of brightnesses which her grandmother had described; and all the darknesses, the dangerous things, the unpleasant things, the depressing and frightening things had never been quite real to her.... So that in the end *nothing* had remained real, and she had waited. Waited for reality indubitably to appear.

Boys had made love to her. They had tried desperately to force her to their purposes.... And she had known that this was the sort of things boys did to other girls; that such actions were more or less general; but rather unconsciously and vaguely she had felt, too, that all this had nothing to do with the brightnesses which her grandmother had endlessly described to her for years. From the time she was able to understand words and utter a few; perhaps even before that time her grandmother had held her and whispered these things, and the words had beaten themselves into her plastic young subconscious, and made records there, even before she knew language; records that still remained.

Much as it distressed her now to realize it she saw that this had been a very bad thing, despite the fact that the motives of those around her had been kindly.... But they had lied ... misrepresented ... distorted the facts; made life appear completely out of joint with itself, so that she was never prepared; was not even now prepared, to live realistically.

She could recall the scandals that had frequently occurred when she was a child; in which neighbors, friends, relatives and acquaintances occasionally became involved. These, when they were explained to her, had always been deftly touched over ... glozed upon.

"Why did Mr. Watkins shoot his wife?"

"Because, dear, he found her with Mr. Gunderson."

"Well, what was Mr. Gunderson doing?"

"He was kissing her."

And this they had felt was "giving the child the facts instead of refusing to answer her questions and thus forcing her to seek information elsewhere."

... How times had changed, even in the short span of her memories. Now, a mere *affaire,* between one woman's husband and another man's wife was considered a mild enough thing indeed. Even though most of the country's novelists were still concerned with such matters, decided mutations had occurred—not engendering really a new state of affairs; but rather bringing age-old concepts back into contemporary usage.

Life, she reflected, was like a never-ending pageant which, passing the reviewing stand of Contemporaries went on around the world again to pass the reviewing stand in another age. And the actors changed costumes on the way around. In Nero's day, for instance, ordinary *affaires* between members of the opposite sexes were thought not at all exciting. There had been, however, much tittle tattle upon matters of a more exotic hue.

Then the pageant had moved on. Out of strife and turmoil that had killed off most of the lusty and the brave, had grown a milk and water civilization which mewled about "Vice." The actors in the pageant changed their costumes and grew more furtive; until at last it became almost taboo to even mention the facts of life. Children were no longer even told where babies came from.

And then again the pageant had passed the reviewing post of the Contemporary. Poets and novelists had grown daring again. They hinted that wives were not always faithful to their husbands. Then the World War and mental anarchy.... Terrific reaction. And now the pageant had come around again bedecked in purple costumes resembling those which had passed in review before Heliogabalus.

How much better if the poets and novelists frankly went into matters so long tabooed; handling them in such a manner as to make contemporary life patterns clear.... How extraordinary that neither Miriam nor she had suspected.... And they should have, Elaine now saw. They were not in ignorance of such matters.

She stirred restlessly in bed. Wished that she had the strength, the energy, or at least the impulse to get up and dress ... go out and play tennis.

If Hyde would only come home and play a game of tennis with her; it might restore everything to its old balance.... But no, it couldn't either; for Hyde could not look into her eyes; and she could not look into his. Fortunate, indeed, it was, that he did not guess ... that he had done something which made him think that the error, the remissness ... the impasse to which they had come was his fault.

... But this thing could not go on. It must be stopped in some way. Poor Miriam. How was *she to* get out of it?

If it were only possible decorously, and without great complication, to escape from the accursed house. There was something overpowering about it; about the servants, everything. It was impossible to guess how much the servants knew; how much they suspected. But they knew and suspected to some extent, and for that reason had a furtive, secretive air. They spoke in soft, unsure tones ... crept silently about the house.

It was, Elaine told herself, a horrible house. Its deceit was monstrous. It looked so much like one of those bright, fairylike homes which her grandmother had once described. Yet it held none of the brightnesses that such a house should hold.

A reason for her lying so much abed occurred to her in new perspective. She was retreating; fleeing from life. She was hiding in bed trying to throw herself back in time and space to her grandmother's lap. She could not, she would not; she dare not— she had no equipment for going ahead into life with responsibilities of her own; cut off from everything but her own initiative. Heretofore her life had been lived more or less for her by others. At home her parents had lived it for her; at school her instructors had done her thinking for her ... passed it on to her in the form of sweetened lozenges which she swallowed by memorizing them, until the whole process meant nothing at all.

From Maine to California; from Reno to El Paso ... east and west, north and south, institutions of "learning" were turning out graduates who, in general, all thought the same about most things. Few of them could think independently, because none of them knew anything that everybody hadn't been taught according to the wholesale standardization of stereotyped universal education ... and almost all of what they were taught was bosh, she could see that all too plainly now. College was merely an intricate extension of grandmother's lap.

She must, she knew, make some sort of decision in regard to her marriage. But it was so hard to make a decision. Withheld from sensual sweets for years by some queer idealistic mental quirk, the sweets were overpoweringly repulsive now that they had come at last ... now that she had discovered, with Miriam's help, that the bodily organism held potentialities far more degrading than she had ever before imagined.

... If, she thought, she had only at an early age been gradually inducted into the pleasures of love as most normal girls nowadays were. A sweetheart or two at high school.... A few discreet lovers at college ... that was the healthy, normal thing to do. Or if only she had come upon a novel, even the year before, explaining her present situation ... illuminating it; she might know what to do.... But there were still the censors.... Some of them kindly disposed, like her grandmother, insisting that life be twisted out of all proportion to itself for the good of the young ... what the young really needed was facts. Unvarnished, uninhibited, uncensored facts. The problem which now existed between Hyde and herself was, she knew, a fairly general one ... such situations, in America, were everywhere on the increase ... and as against them was raised only a countrywide "Shush!" ... instead of wholesome information.

She decided she must have a talk with Miriam. It must end. She must get back to what was natural for a woman.... Even yet it might be possible that Hyde and she ... now that she knew what was wrong with her ... what threatened her.... Perhaps, with his understanding and help, after a time....

Upon this reflection she drifted off into a light sleep.

# CHAPTER ELEVEN
## *WHOSE FAULT?*

MIRIAM WAS subject to migraine headaches; had been since birth; had inherited the tendency from her father, who had died at the age of forty-nine of cerebral hemorrhage.

... Migraine had a devastating effect upon the personality, not unlike a mild form of epilepsy. When an attack came on—and when they came they lasted for from three to ten days—it arrived with a dull, dry numbing headache, which froze up the thinking faculties; caused a dull expression to replace her usually bright and vivid one. Her perfect white skin became grayish. Her usually bright eyes were dulled. Her whole physical organism underwent metamorphosis. Gradually the dull, dry headache which seemed to freeze up her mind and body advanced to a sharp, acute headache which all but drove her crazy with pain. When the attack had advanced to this stage she walked the floor; strove to put herself into all manner of positions to ease the hideous pain in her head.

Usually courageous and fearless she became the veriest of cowards, faced by the threat of an attack and its following pain. She would let no one come near her or see her after an attack began; not even her mother. Servants brought what little she could eat or drink to her room, wherein she always stayed, incommunicado until the attacks were over. She had a horror of even the servants seeing her at such times. When they entered her room with a tray, she stepped into the bathroom and remained in hiding until they had put down the tray and gone.... Crying often, helplessly, and shaken with strange fears and dreads against which she had adequate defenses at all other times. Her whole personality underwent, temporarily, such a radical change that she was almost unrecognizable even to herself. No matter how greatly she might care about something shortly before an attack, it all passed from her mind during the attack, and she became craven, beaten, hopeless; afraid even of strange sounds in her own home; more afraid of crying out in alarm, or of going to anyone for comfort.

Aware of this phase of Miriam's character Elaine was not surprised or distressed when, as they were driving back from a matinee in town, in Elaine's car, Miriam, who had been silent and pale during the ride out from Manhattan, said in a tense, tremulous voice:

"Please tell the chauffeur to stop at my place and drop me off."

Elaine did not remonstrate; she knew that it was no use to ask to stay with her until she felt better. She merely nodded and patted Miriam's hand. This brought no warm flush of happiness to Miriam, as usually it did. She gazed palely out of the window and ignored the pat. Elaine, this time, felt strangely nonplused. It was as though Miriam with a weary gesture put her out of her life forever ... as though she wished never again to see her or hear of her ... as though she had lost completely all interest in her.

Elaine sat stricken and silent in the car, though she knew well enough, from past experiences, that it was all a temporary matter; that Miriam, after the attack, would be her old self ... more tender and understanding than before.

But she sat now silent and stricken, a vacant stare upon her face, staring out of the car window. Elaine felt strangely afraid and alone. It was as if she had taken on powers of invisibility; as though there were nobody present but Miriam.

The car turned in at Miriam's home and she got out. Did not even say good-bye. Did not turn as she hurried toward the house. Merely walked off, a slender woebegone figure.

As the car drove on after leaving Miriam's place, Elaine felt increasingly depressed. It was growing dark. There were low clouds overhead which made it even darker than usual at this time of night.

A new apprehension was upon her. She realized, for the first time, that she was changing radically. Fright shook her deeply at this dread thought.... To change utterly; to be not at all one's old self. To enter upon a new order of life. To take on a new personality. One which might forever prevent her from getting into contact with the brightnesses for which she was always unconsciously hunting.

Collateral to this thought rising terror took her. She was feeling, she realized, at the abrupt defection of Miriam, all the intensity of emotional despair that she might be expected to feel over the sudden defection of Hyde.

This would never do, she told herself frantically; this *must not be*. It would forever separate her from the brightnesses:

The car rounded a bend in the road, and, for a moment, the house was visible, in all of its deceitful perfection. Over it hung the heavy, leaden clouds, menacingly. Surrounding it were the stiff and straight trees. From approaching it Elaine shrank back ... but she dared not go to her parents' home and face their endless, puzzled questions. Somehow a little something had leaked out ... probably through the servants' grapevine of gossip which covered that section of Long Island. She must go to the accursed house and its malicious spell which it seemed to cast over everyone in it to such a degree that even the servants felt it; even the chauffeur's dog, which often howled strangely at night.

Now they turned into the private driveway and started toward the house. Elaine thought with sharp curiosity of Max, Miriam's chauffeur. People still talked about Max and Miriam ... which was a very good thing, on the whole, since it kept their minds busy in another direction. But, after all, it *was* a fact that Miriam led a strangely isolated and mysterious life. When Miriam was at home and her mother was not, often there was Max on the place. Handsome, virile, uncommunicative ... with an air of refinement and culture not usually evidenced by chauffeurs.

With reluctance she entered the house. The dark wainscoting in the hall had its usual depressing effect upon her. The deathly stillness and silence of the place affected her so sharply that she could have turned and fled down the private road to, she could not imagine where.

There was someone in the living room. She entered, glad of the fact that there was someone there. It was so dark in the room that she did not at first see who it was. When he turned and the faint light from the window illuminated his profile she saw that it was Hyde. Affectedly she said:

"Well, you're quite a stranger."

They had been married for nearly a month now and at least two nights out of three he did not come home at all. As though to equal her own interjection he drawled:

"Where's Miriam?"

It was not to annoy her, really, that he had asked this, though he realized there was that in his tone which he had not intended to put there which seemed to give his words a wry twist. He really wanted to know where Miriam was. For days he had thrown his mind against the mystery, trying to find the key to unlock his way to a position of complete power over Miriam, so that he might force her to things of which he dreamed.

Elaine took off her things and sat down near him.

"Miriam and I went to see 'Lady Obey.' She was taken ill on the way back and I left her at her home."

" 'Ill?' "

"Yes. Nothing serious. She's subject to migraine headaches. She'll be over it in a few days."

"Then she'll come back to practically live here again?"

"Do you mind, Hyde?"

"Not in the least, if you don't."

"Why should I mind?"

"You seem to be the only one who doesn't suspect that Miriam and I are having a love *affaire* right under your nose and in your house."

" 'My house!' "

"Certainly. I explained to you that father had the deed made out in your name. It was his wedding gift."

She gasped:

"My God! Is this place really mine?"

"Of course. And all the land around it, so that nobody can build and interfere with our view; and all the furniture in it—the Packard is yours, too."

"Is it all insured?"

"Fire insurance, you mean?"

"Yes."

"Of course it's insured; but why do you ask that?"

"Because I'd like to burn it all up and everything in it."

Jerking into an erect sitting posture, he said, with a curious intonation:

"Would you?"

"Yes, I would."

"Well, Elaine, so would I."

They sat wordlessly for a time, the idea having warmed to life some of the feeling that had once been between them.

"Of course, Elaine, I'm not quite serious.... We couldn't burn it up. There might be complications, unless we waived the insurance.... And there'd be no need to destroy it anyway—we could just go away."

"Where would we go?"

"I don't know, Elaine; there's no place on earth I really want to go."

"Where do you go, when you don't stay here?"

"To a small apartment in town that I've had for a long time."

"Really! I'd like to see it."

"Would you?"

"Yes. I'd like to see it *right now.* I'd like to get away from this damned house."

"I'm sorry about the house—but don't forget that I begged you to express yourself about it before it was built; but you told me to go ahead—and I had no ideas in particular. I asked Dad to take care of it ... and finally, though he handled the financial details, the other matters were left to your mother and father. Maybe that's what's wrong with it. It doesn't reflect *our personality.* It's a hybrid house. Composite and synthetic. Maybe, in fact, the architect was some sort of psychopathic specimen. Now that I come to think of it it's entirely possible that *that's* what's wrong. Architecture is an art form.... The only one, in fact, that impresses me. In any art form one must be able to sense something of one's own personality in it to enjoy it fully. Take the weird quality in Tschaikowsky's music ... it does something to you. Read Oscar Wilde's 'Dorian Gray' and you have queer creeps for days. Pierre Louy's poems ... 'The Songs of Bilitis'.... Praxiteles: there's something about the 'Cnidian Venus,' that hits you in a strange way; and if you study it, you can't explain to yourself what the feeling is, and yet.... To say nothing of painting and the things you often get from a canvas that aren't obviously implicit.

"Think what the Moors managed to express in some of their architecture: you all but turn away in embarrassment, and yet you...."

"I know what you mean," she cut in. "I've felt it all my life too."

What had once been between them was coming more and more to life. It had grown darker outside. Now they could hardly see each other. But they were greatly aware of each other there in the dark. Aware, too, of the strange and clammy waiting quality in the house. Aware of minute sounds somewhere in the house.... The servants, and the strange spell that was always over them, as though they, too, were conscious of inhabiting a house with a dark curse upon it. He went on affirmatively, as though talking mostly to himself:

"... Yes, an artist can work into any art form things which are felt by, and which react upon almost any sensitive person ... upon almost anyone except art critics who look for academic evidences confirming whatever theories they may happen to hold in respect to the art form under examination."

"Yes," she nodded sympathetically, and wished to draw closer to him there in the dark for protection against the enfoldment of the house. It was as though the house contracted a little at a time there in the dark; might, conceivably, crush them both.

"I hadn't told them to get dinner," he informed her. "I didn't know whether you were coming or not, and I wasn't sure whether I'd stay or not. What do you say we both get out of here right away?"

"Let's."

"We could have dinner in town.... Go to a show. Go somewhere else afterward. Anywhere you like."

"... And stay in your apartment in town tonight?"

"Would you like to?"

She caught the undertone in his voice. She was at once afraid; but there was no alternative.

"Yes...." She whispered unsteadily.

"Well, come on then."

When they were in the car, riding back to town, she felt strangely exuberant and happy; and he chatted amiably:

"... Know what we'll do after the show? We'll go see Thurston. He'll amuse you."

"The novelist, Thurston?"

"Yes, the one who wrote 'Forward Lass'."

"Yes, you hear all sorts of things about him. He doesn't run with the pack; and he writes too uncomfortably well to please his colleagues ... even though he does write always on themes that are an abomination."

"Sickening sex stuff ..." she supplied.

"Exactly. He's completely non persona grata with the crowd ... that's what makes him interesting. Met him in a bar the other night. Had his sixteen-year-old son with him. You never see him without his son."

"You have a life all your own that I haven't any part in, haven't you, Hyde?"

"... Well—!"

"Yes, I know; don't say it. It's my fault, of course. We got off to a wrong start, didn't we?"

"*That* was *my* fault."

"I'm not so sure, Hyde."

They were aware that awkward restraint had intruded and frosted the atmosphere which had been a moment before so cozy. They had each remembered something. Desperately she threw herself against the hiatus, determined to smash through it. A few minutes before she had been almost happy and care-free. She must try to hold on to that mood, she inwardly decided. They *both* must try. He had forgotten himself in what he had been talking of. She urged:

"Go on and tell me more about him."

"… Well, I think he can write entertainingly because he never learned anything … almost never went to school. Ran away from home when he was very young; managed in some astonishing fashion to make his own way. He hides behind literary agents, never sees any publishers, book reviewers, other authors or 'intel-lectuals'.… None of that artificial group of poseurs. He spends his time almost wholly, when he's not working, with his son. They associate with all sorts of people except the artificial ones.…

"His son likes hot dogs, radios, motion pictures, and every-thing that the son of a novelist ought not to like.… So his father likes these things too. His greatest pleasure in life is to watch his son having fun out of the simplest of things.

"He's never tried to teach his son anything.… Didn't send him to school.

"… Thurston hasn't any belief in anything; especially not in what's called 'Human Knowledge'. He says it's his ambition to find out something … but he can't find anything real or true except his son; so he tries to learn the secrets of life from his son; for he says the boy has the secret, in that he knows how to live and be continually entertained and happy. He studies his son night and day with far more diligence than most novelists devote to studying artifacts."

"But his wife? What about her?"

"Oh, they were divorced before the war. She found a man still attached to a little money and left Thurston. He says for a time his son and he faced starvation … and he was sick; but they were happy, he claims, even then. He doesn't seem to be bitter about his wife. He's grateful to her … she did, he says, one splendid thing for their son. She passed on to the child none of her own characteristics."

"He certainly sounds interesting; but why in Heaven's name does he write such dreadful trash—that is, provided what I've heard about his work is true."

"That's the funniest part of it … he claims he does it only because that's the only sort of thing that always has a steady sale in every age. He does it, in short, to buy whatever his son wants to amuse himself with, and appears to have no interest in his work aside from that … though there are spots in all his books, bad as most of them are that—well, you'll probably read one of them after you meet him, and then you'll see what I mean."

He was silent now, as the car sped along. After a time she prompted:

"You'd like to have a son, wouldn't you, Hyde?"

"Maybe *that's* it," he said, as though speaking to himself.

" 'Maybe that's what?' "

He turned upon her in some puzzlement.

"I don't know exactly what I meant, Elaine; it was vague in my own mind. Only—well, what *is* there in life?"

"I know what you mean, perfectly, Hyde; maybe that's the only brightness that—"

" 'Brightness?' "

"I can't explain, Hyde."

"You don't need to explain one thing, Elaine; so don't worry about it. I know well enough that you wouldn't welcome the thought of motherhood with any—"

"I'm afraid you're right, Hyde."

"Well, anyway, something touched us tonight didn't it, dear; I hope it lasts a while longer."

" 'Touched us?' " she echoed.

"Yes, it is as though something had been turned off, or turned on … I dont' know which."

Elaine was thoughtful. She remembered Miriam. Miriam was at home, her whole mind and spirit temporarily different from what they usually were. Whatever her mind held at most times, it did not hold now.

"Hyde, do you believe in mental telepathy?"

"I don't know. There appears to be something in it; but of course nobody knows."

"Do you think that one with a strong mind might affect, telepathically, over long periods, perhaps several years, the mind of another?"

"I doubt it. Surely the experiment's been tried often enough, and the results are usually negative I'm informed."

"Yes, but suppose one person had some sort of telepathic control over another of which they themselves were not aware? That is, while it might be true that experiments in mental telepathy fail, it may be equally true that a person unconsciously and, without any thought of doing so deliberately, can control another person in some respect or to some extent."

"That's the only sort of mental telepathy I *could* believe in."

"It does seem fantastic though, doesn't it," she ended lamely.

"Rather," he agreed; "still…."

# CHAPTER TWELVE
## *THE LOVELIEST MISTRESS*
## *OF THEM ALL*

I T WAS nearly two o'clock in the morning when they got to Hyde's little apartment after a visit with Thurston.

Elaine was in a gay mood. It was impossible to spend any time with Thurston without attaining good spirits. His depths of cynicism and carefree pessimism, a bit overdone, conduced inevitably to a feeling of lightness when one's own troubles were cast against such a background. Thurston's philosophy, she saw, was an obvious one. Unlike most cynics and pessimists he looked, not for the worst, but for things that were so much worse than anything which could possibly happen, that whatever *did* happen came as a pleasurable surprise.

She examined the hideout delightedly.

"Why, this is swell, Hyde—but you've spoiled it forever—bringing your wife here. You'll never know now when I may not drop in on you."

He grinned boyishly, and with a singular lightheartedness that she had not observed in him since the wedding.

Sitting down on the long divan in the living room she sank into its depths and accepted a cigarette.

"What's the matter with us tonight, Elaine? Have we gone mad? We seem to have changed completely."

"Maybe it's knowing we don't have to sleep in that house."

"Yes, Elaine, perhaps; and yet there's nothing wrong with the house, really. I suppose it's just that the first night there—!"

"… There may be a lot in that," she agreed frowning slightly.

"Still," he continued, "I think it happened before that. Some sort of change came over me as soon as we became engaged. When we were married it was as though—well, I simply can't explain it."

"I feel like a different person, too, tonight: I've felt this way occasionally before, as though heavy things had been lifted off."

Sitting down upon the floor at her feet he gazed up at her. She felt afraid, knowing what he expected. She must, she told herself firmly, try to coincide with his wishes…. And now that she came to think of it directly she felt no great reluctance to do so … not so great a reluctance as she had felt that first time when she had called him in from the tennis court and up to her room. As though he were reading her thoughts he remarked:

"Do you know that you and I haven't played tennis together once since we were married."

"No, that's right, we haven't."

"I've got everything we'd need here, except suitable apparel for you. What do you say we send out to the house for something for you to wear and play over on the Columbia courts tomorrow—they're not far from here."

"I'd like that, Hyde."

He stared off across the room vacantly, and smiled as though he were thinking of matters piquant.

"Dare I risk a penny on your thoughts?" she hazarded. He broke into an easy laugh:

"Oh sure—they're not shocking … particularly. I was just thinking of Thurston … the rage he went into over nudism!

Elaine laughed too.

"You can't blame him. His reasons, it seems to me, were valid ones. It *would* ruin the sex story."

"But he was wrong," Hyde declared hotly, "in most of what he said. I could follow him when he said that it would ruin his racket because if people got accustomed to seeing each other nude they'd lose all the old childish prurience toward sex built into their minds in this country for years. They'd take sex and nudity so matter-of-factly that 'immorality' would practically vanish and we'd know it no more than the Indians did before the white missionaries came; but when he says no woman is as pretty nude as she is clothed...."

Elaine blushed.

"I love your ability still to blush," Hyde approved.

"Do you think I'm prettier nude than—"

"Yes, and—"

"Go on, say it—you were going to say: 'You, and lots of others,' weren't you?"

"I guess I was," he confessed sheepishly.

"How many others, Hyde?"

"Do you mind?"

"Not in the least."

"... Oh, I suppose there were a hundred or so, off and on."

"How many in this apartment?"

"Oh, not so many here—there were quite a lot at school."

"... And were all of them prettier nude than—"

"Good Heaven's no! Thurston was right so far as the majority are concerned, but—you, for instance, pink and white and golden; with big, blue eyes for counterpoint!"

She smiled friendlily.

"You're sure you don't mind my talking like that, Elaine?"

"No."

"In a way it's sort of queer that you don't." He looked unhappy. She felt a touch of chill and apprehension. Would she be able, she wondered, after all, to go through with this? So far as she felt at the moment she was quite sure that she could—but on those former occasions; the only two former occasions that there had been between them....! It was very strange, she thought, that she didn't feel that way now; but she *might,* so soon as he made any direct overtures, and for that reason she was afraid though she did not really feel sickened or repelled as she had previously. If only Miriam could be wrong as to what was to follow!

"I'm getting morbid again," he diagnosed. "We need a brace of cocktails."

"Before retiring!"

"Well, highballs then."

"All right—but don't let's get drunk again."

"Don't worry, Elaine. I won't. And I won't let you. I'm dreadfully sorry about—"

"I wish you'd stop apologizing for that."

Rising, he mixed highballs for them. As they sipped he said:

"Sure you wouldn't prefer to stay here alone tonight and let me run along to a hotel?"

"No, I wouldn't prefer that at all."

"You mean—?"

"Of course."

"... Angel!"

Still sitting before her upon the floor he raised her skirts and kissed dimpled, rounded knees. Over him there was a new tenderness toward her; something approaching what he had formerly felt in respect to her. She put out a hand and ruffled his hair. He *was* likeable, she decided; though she would have preferred that he had not kissed her knees. It reminded her too much of something, even when they were kissed while she had sheer silk stockings on. Now that she *was* reminded of this something she became thoughtful and over her there crept a feeling too familiar to be comfortable. She gazed down at him speculatively. She *must*, somehow, she sternly scolded within herself, get over such notions; learn to enjoy or at least to bear with equanimity, the more natural things. For a moment she felt provoked and annoyed at the thought of Miriam, and inclined to blame her for everything that had happened; yet when she thought of her directly, alone in her room, suffering like the devil, it was hard really to feel angry with her.

Lightly she said, glancing at the clock on an end-table:

"It's nearly three. I'm getting tired. If we're going to play tennis tomorrow...."

"Yes," he agreed, a trifle nervously.

"You take the bedroom. I'll sleep out here on the divan. There's a door into the bathroom from the bedroom; and that door there also leads to it from this room."

She debated for a moment; touched again with the fear of not being able to go through with things. Said at last, without meeting his eyes:

"All right. If you don't mind."

She knew that he was disappointed. Getting up she moved toward the bedroom. He rose and stood by her side for a moment. Put his arm tenderly around her. Said:

"You're sweet, Elaine. You're so different, down here, from what you ever have been before, anywhere."

Patting his hand she went on into the bedroom.... Thoughtfully undressed. Once she smiled to herself. It *was* droll, now that she came to think of it. Other women who came here—yet, his own wife—!

She noticed the full-length mirror set into the bathroom door.... When she had finished undressing, remembered that she had no nightgown. Opening a drawer she found several sets of clean pyjamas. She took out a pair of blue ones, with a large initial embroidered in silk upon the top piece. Putting the pyjamas down upon the bed she turned again toward the mirror. Surveyed herself.

" '... Pink and white and gold ... with big, blue eyes.' " Yes, it was quite true. With the light still on went over and lay down upon the bed. She could still see herself in the mirror.... At full length; all soft curves and seductive contours.... All pinkness and whiteness and goldenness.... Warmth ... fragrance and femaleness.

There was a small lacquer stand near the bed. On it was a lacquer box of cigarettes, and a lighter. Lighting a cigarette she lay carelessly in the warm room, puffing at the cigarette and pondering fearfully; watching herself with a certain voluptuous appreciation in the mirror.

She could hear Hyde moving around in the next room. Finally he tapped at the door. She started, violently, and glanced around, frantic, for something to pull over her; then forced herself not to cover herself. In a small voice she called out:

"Yes? ..."

"I'm sorry to trouble you, dear, but my pyjamas are in there. I forgot. If the light's turned off, it's all right; I can find them in the dark ... and I want to get some covers out of the closet in there."

Tremblingly she said:

"It's all right, come in."

Opening the door he stepped into the room. Stopped a moment in surprise, finding the lights on. His gaze went, not toward her, but toward the mirror. She saw him stiffen, then slowly swing around to look at her.

Moving slowly toward her he knelt down. Said:

"You're the loveliest ef them all."

Something about the simple statement, uttered with a fervency that testified to its sincerity deeply touched her. When he leaned over and kissed her passionately upon the lips she responded. Threw her arms up and around his neck.

When his hands tested the softness of her warm, fragrant flesh everywhere she was a trifle frightened, but did not object. His virile, strong arms, surrounding her, holding her in a tight and meaningful grip, frightened and distracted her so that she had the impulse to cry out—but did not.

"I love you ..." he whispered vibrantly; and, for the first time in her life the words did something to her. Relaxing, she was no longer afraid.

"Do you want me to go, Elaine?"

She hesitated, but found herself saying:

"No."

"Shall I turn out the lights?"

She remembered the mirror on the bathroom door. Twisted around so that she could see into it. What she saw stirred her profoundly. It was as though they were another two ... not Elaine and Hyde.... That lovely girl subjugated. Held in such a purposeful, resolute embrace by the strong male creature.

"No," she directed, "leave them on." She watched the glass in terrified but at the same time delighted fascination.

# CHAPTER THIRTEEN
## *WHAT'S MIRIAM UP TO?*

W ESLEY VANNER, Elaine's father, stood before the mirror in his bathroom, engaged about the one thing left in his life that moved him deeply: pimple popping.

Sixty-five years of age, he appeared well preserved. A trifle stocky, he was tall enough to carry it gracefully. He had still most of his hair; but it had become grayish without turning white and had, lately, a tendency to scraggle. He stood erect. His eyes were gray, flecked with dark lights like the glints in granite. Clad now in gray bathrobe, gray slippers and black pyjamas, he leaned far forward over the washstand and peered closely at the mirror. His arms were twisted into grotesque positions, as he concentrated carefully upon a pimple that had defied him for several minutes. With great delicacy and exactness he got his fingers placed, and squeezed. At last the pimple yielded.

Though he appeared to be strong and healthy, at first glance, he actually was not. The past four years had done subtle damage which had not yet had time much to affect his strong outer shell.

At college he had played football auspiciously well. In the years after college he had gone in much for horseback riding, golfing, and, curiously enough, skating. Never at any time of his life given much to drinking, and leading, from force of habit, the sort of athletic life he had been taught in college, he had developed—through having benefited by this one thing that a young man may learn at college—into a very healthy person.

The first two or three years of the depression had all but finished him. Now, however, he was resigned. He had lost interest in practically everything except pimple popping. Hyde's father had loaned him sufficient to carry his investments over until the investment market began to thaw. There was nothing much for him to worry about—except the painful boils, which sometimes overtook him because of an unfortunate habit of eating cake and candy which he had formed a year before. When he went to bed at night, after popping his pimples, he was a sight to behold, with the patches of iodine over his face. Not that there were many pimples ... nor were they sufficient to make him a repulsive sight—especially if he each night took care of them.

As he worked now, his mind wandered mistily back over his life as it always did at this time of night when he stood before the mirror thus engaged.

His life had started comfortably and now it appeared that it would end in about the same way, relatively speaking. His father before him had been wealthy. There had been the school years, packed with good fun, not all of it too clean. There had been a mild period of cabaret carousing after college; and then the entry into his father's investment banking business.... Followed by his marriage to Amy. This, he congratulated himself, had been one of the wisest moves of his entire career. He frowned a bit and missed a pimple when he recalled, in this connection, that his marriage to Amy hadn't, after all, been his own doing. He had, at the time, he now recollected, balked. It had been his father's doing. That gentleman had said simply:

"Look here, Wesley ... unless Amy is downright repulsive to you—and I don't see how she possibly could be, she's a very attractive girl—you ought to marry her whether you love her or not. Love should be kept in the corner, like the cocktail shaker, and brought out on merry occasions. You can have any number of discreet love *affaires* after you're married; but if you marry for love—!"

At that time Wesley had considered his father's advice over-cynical; yet, Amy *was* attractive. Her father was economically sound, her social position impeccable ... her family one of the oldest in America.... So he had married her wholly because his father had wished him to. He had sworn to Amy at the time that he loved her. Though there had never in all their married years been the slightest mention of it between them, Wesley was pretty sure that there had been motives of the same sort behind her acceptance of him, though she had sworn that she loved him.

Their probable lack of love, at the outset, had developed and ripened into a conjugality far more workable and sensible than what had developed with most of his male friends of the time who actually *had* married for love. Most of them had gone through one or more divorces; and all of them led miserable married lives, chasing the will-o'-the-wisp of marital love, instead of following the cogent English custom of marrying for sound reasons.

A rapport had developed between Amy and him which was neither love nor the lack of it. Something complacent and peaceful and eminently satisfactory to them both. That she cared for him, deeply, now, he knew; and he cared more for her than for any living being; more, even, than he cared for Elaine, or himself. They grumbled at each other, bickered mildly, and were almost totally undemonstrative—but Amy's death, he knew, would kill him; and his death, he was comfortably certain, would kill her.... And they had both lived long, comfortable, happy lives. Neither was afraid of death, or life—they were afraid only of one thing— losing each other.

About Elaine, Wesley felt now comfortable and happy. She had been urged into the same sort of marriage. It, too, in all probability, he thought, would ripen into a thing solid and tenable; far more so than the hysterical marriages for love which ended in the divorce courts, if the participators were sensitive; or, which was far worse, ended in one of those hideous endurance tests or masochistic marathons which Americans called a "Successful Marriage." He was infinitely glad that there had never been a son. He wouldn't have known what on earth to do with one in times like the present.

He was comfortably aware of being surrounded by reasonable luxury, when so many of his colleagues had passed through frightful mutations and ended in poverty. The period of anxiety, for him, after Hyde's father's help, had definitely ended. He had lost millions; his career was over. All that he would do now would be to preserve what he could of the family fortune and pass it on to Elaine. He had lost much, and they must even now be very careful of expenditures. There was no longer any private yacht. There were only two cars; one for the family and one for the servants. And there were left only four servants. But at least he still had his home, he reflected with satisfaction, and there was no likelihood now that he would lose it, or lack the means to keep it running fairly well, if they were a bit careful. Fortunate indeed, he had been, he assured himself, when one considered the plight of his fellows. Suddenly Amy called out to him. They each occupied a private suite, between which there were connecting doors. Grinning a bit sheepishly to himself he walked toward Amy's suite. In the first years of the depression, when he had fought like a madman to keep from losing his millions, there had been black despairs after hopeless defeats … and during those times Amy had conceived a fear that he might commit suicide, as several of their friends and acquaintances similarly placed had done. When he was long alone, or engaged at night silently in the bathroom, he knew that she was again seized with the fear that he might be preparing to take poison, or cut his throat.

This fear in her now, he knew, was not a very real one; it was merely the hangover phobia that had come to her as a result of the trying first two years of the depression. He knew that she would get over it in time, now that they were comfortably situated and needed no longer to worry.

When he entered her bedroom he found her sitting up in bed, anxious eyed and white. She was still pretty. Six years his junior she had taken excellent and expensive care of herself. She asked sharply:

"What were you doing?"

"Popping pimples." Watching her eyes he saw the fear die out of them; saw it replaced by the mildly provoked feeling that always followed the dispelling of her fears for his safety.

"You look like a leopard," she accused.

He sat down on the bed smiling.

She relaxed. Lay back on her pillows. He smiled and patted her hand.

Her hair had been excellently dyed, so that none of its grayness showed.... Facials had left her skin amazingly youthful. Her figure was still slim. She had deeply blue eyes, and her features were impressive in an almost classic way which would not dim even with old age. Though he had, in former years, enjoyed many extra-marital *affaires,* he had never found another woman whom he considered in any way more attractive than Amy ... and she, though aware of some of his *affaires,* had never objected, because she had seemed intuitively to sense that she was getting no *real* competition. And she, too, had had several lovers, he knew; but he had not worried. Their tenure had always been short, and she had in no way changed toward him during these temporary infatuations.

"There's nothing to worry about," he again assured her. Usually, by this time, the worry would completely have faded from her face; but it did not. They knew each other so well that they could all but read each other's minds.

"What is it, Amy?"

She knew better than to evade the issue. He would know that something other than her phobia about the possibility of his committing suicide was perplexing her tonight. No use to tell him that there was not.

"I'm a bit worried about Elaine and—"

" 'Elaine!' Why! What's wrong?" He too was concerned now and leaned forward on the bed.

"I don't know what it is, Wes, but there's something strange going on there. Neither Elaine nor Hyde has been home for five days."

"What! Why! Where are they! You don't think—!"

"No, there's nothing like that—they're seen around town together so I know they're all right…. But ever since their marriage—" she broke off in puzzlement.

"Yes, what is it?" he prompted.

"Well, for one thing, something strange happened on their wedding night. I haven't the faintest idea what—I've heard talk from the servants. I know that there was some kind of a fight."

" 'A fight!' " He was aghast.

"… Well I don't know whether it was between Hyde and Elaine, or—"

"Who else could have been involved?"

"Miriam Atwell went there at two or three o'clock in the morning."

"She did! What for?"

"That I don't know."

"Did you ask Elaine about it?"

"She's never been here *once* since they were married."

"She hasn't!"

"Not once. She keeps calling up and saying she'll be over—but when she calls I can tell that there's something wrong, and that she doesn't come because she doesn't want to be questioned.... I had made up my mind to take matters in hand and go and get out of her what's wrong; but as I tell you, they don't either one of them go home any more, and I don't know where to reach them."

"I don't see much to worry about in all that, frankly."

"No," she conceded, brows drawn together in perplexity: "there isn't much to be seen on the surface. Today Miriam came here. She has spells when she gets sick for four or five days at a time. She'd just come out of one of these spells. She was pale as a ghost, and I never saw her so excited before. She wanted to know where Elaine and Hyde were, and when I told her I didn't know I could see that she didn't believe me. She'd been trying every way to find them."

"Well, what do you think is wrong?"

"That's just it. I don't know. But I could see from Miriam's attitude that there *was* something definitely wrong somewhere."

"Why didn't you question, Miriam?"

"I couldn't bring myself to. I've always been sort of afraid of her."

" 'Afraid of her!' Why she's only a slip of a girl, and—"

"Well, I don't mean, precisely, afraid of her; only sort of baffled by her—although goodness knows she's always been lovely to me, except today she—was rather cool and, as I say, obviously didn't believe me. The servants over at Elaine's and Hyde's place said that she had carefully questioned them as to Elaine's and Hyde's whereabouts; and they further said that she'd been staying there a lot ever since the wedding … all night. There's something funny about those servants. About that whole house. They're perfectly good servants … excellent references, came from a good agency. But they've changed in some way since they went to work there. I talked to them before the house was opened; and I talked to them yesterday … and they were furtive, secretive … strange. In fact the whole house gave me the creeps."

Wesley reached forward and put his hand gently to her forehead. She protested:

"Wes! If you go and get that fever thermometer and stick it into my mouth I'll simply chew it up and spit it out at you. I've *not* got any fever. I'm *not* talking this way because I'm delirious."

"No, you're not," he agreed with gentle concern. "You're perfectly cool. But I think you're attaching entirely too much importance to—"

"I know. There's no one thing, really, to attach any significance to, Wes … it's just the whole business. That is, ever since the marriage, they've both acted so strangely. Never see anybody … never do anything you might expect a newly married couple to do.… It's all so—queer!" She uttered the last word despairingly as though it were not at all the word to fit the case but the only one she could on the spur of the moment find in her mind.

"It is kind of funny," he concurred, scratching his head thoughtfully, and yawning at the same time, plainly evidencing a wish to be concerned, since she was concerned; but a wish toward this end not nearly so strong as his wish to go to bed and to sleep.

"I don't think we should have given Miriam such a free hand, Wes."

"Why not? Neither Elaine nor Hyde wanted to be bothered with the details. Miriam seemed quite taken with the idea of exercising her decorative flare without having to worry about the cost for a change. Winton Hall was a labor of love on her part. Besides, I'm no hand at that sort of thing … and at that time you were deep in that psychiatric clinic benefit."

"Yes, I know," she sighed. "I wish I had had my mind more on my own daughter and less on the daughters of the deserving poor who supposedly needed a free psychiatric clinic so they could have doctors to tell them they were suffering from sex repression instead of finding it out as they would anyhow if left alone."

"I thought Miriam did a marvelous job," he objected, puzzled. "She worked with the architect on the plans of the house, selected the materials, even worked with the interior decorator in detail … she took a big load off our minds and enjoyed doing it—had nothing else to do."

"But why do you suppose Miriam was so insistent that we never tell Hyde or Elaine that she had a hand in building and furnishing their home for them?"

"I don't know, I'm sure, but I don't see—"

"Suppose, Wes, Miriam were in love with Hyde?"

He looked still more deeply puzzled about that.

"Hell, they were in more or less close association long before Hyde proposed to Elaine; they could easily have done something about it then."

"Yes," Amy agreed. "But suppose that Miriam had fallen desperately in love with Hyde, and Hyde didn't return her affections? What then?"

"… Well, Hyde could give her a couple of treatments to ease her through it, couldn't he? I don't see any great cause for alarm in the situation one way or another."

"No," she confessed, "I don't either. That is, I don't *see* any; but I *feel* something. I wish to goodness we hadn't all been so lazy about that house."

"Why worry about that? The responsibility for that—if there's been any harm done and I can't for the life of me see where—is as much Hyde's father's and mother's as ours. In fact, when you come right down to it the responsibility is really Hyde's and Elaine's. They had nothing else on earth to do, why couldn't they have seen to the building and furnishing of their own home?"

"Because Elaine didn't love Hyde enough to care about the place; and Hyde wouldn't have known how to go about such a thing even if he'd wanted to."

"Now that's enough talk for one night. Let's go to bed." She kissed him and he went to his own room.

# CHAPTER FOURTEEN
## *PROVOCATIVE PICTURES*

A S IF UNDER some strange compulsion to do so they went back to the house on Long Island. On the drive out Elaine was silent and morose. In some manner all of the brightness had gone out of the days of truancy from home with Hyde. He, too, seemed affected and thoughtful. As a matter of fact, as he stared glumly and silently out of the car window, he was wondering if Miriam would be there when they got back. He was also wondering why he should hope that she would be. Thinly adumbrated pictures of hectic possibilities between Miriam and himself went through his mind. He blushed and derided himself. The days with Elaine had been sweet; but somehow he was surfeited with that particular sort of sweet; and wanted some bittersweet. Glancing furtively at Elaine he saw that she was abstracted, and wondered of what she was thinking with her brows anxiously knitted in a frown of concentration.

His mind went back to the morning after that first delicious night, when they had felt so happy, so good, so completely right and clean about everything. Elaine, in the midst of their new-found joy, talked vaguely about how wrong Miriam had been, that love could be sweet and fresh the way she had hoped it might be. Then suddenly, she had seemed troubled and a bit saddened about something. He had questioned her about it.

"Hyde, it would make me very happy if you would destroy those photographs of yours."

"What photographs?"

She had flushed deeply, obviously embarrassed. "The ones Miriam found in the library."

He had been frankly puzzled and a bit angered by this vague reference to something she seemed to think he should be ashamed of. He had questioned her about it further, but she had refused to say more, with the maddening attitude that she had indelicately probed into a shameful affair which he refused to admit the existence of out of sheer mortification. He had become more angry and she more stubbornly humble, and the affair was finally dropped. He had not forgotten her puzzling words, however, and as he turned them over and over again in his mind, they began to take on a hazy, indefinite form.

Miriam was undoubtedly up to something. She had some sort of powerful influence over Elaine, a strange power that drew her away from him whenever she was near. He remembered Miriam's curiously defensive attitude that first morning, how it had puzzled and piqued him. Now he felt even more certain that she had some insidious plan in operation of which she was ashamed and apprehensive, with a goal in her sights that she wanted desperately. She was after something, of that he was certain. But what? He was seized with an unwavering determination to find out. He wondered, with a disturbing eagerness, if Miriam would be home when they arrived.

Elaine, too, was wondering if Miriam would be there. Somehow she felt sure that Miriam had wholly recovered from her malaise.

... And she *was* there. Waiting in the hall when they entered. An enigmatical expression upon her pale, finely chiseled features.... Wearing a soft, gray, afternoon frock which displayed to striking advantage all of the lovely contours of her perfect, slim figure.

Hyde said, almost merrily:

"Hello, Miriam."

She nodded and seemed to smile, though he could not be sure of it. She was watching Elaine intently. Elaine said:

"Are you all over it now, dear?"

"Quite." There was an edge of tartness to Miriam's reply. "Where on earth have you two been? Elaine, your mother is worried stiff—and Hyde, your father has 'phoned several times today and asked me to tell you to get in touch with him the minute you came in."

"Thanks, I will," Hyde returned, adding: "It was good of you to see to things while we were gone." He paused and there was an awkward silence between them. He went on:

"If you two will excuse me I'll run along and 'phone."

Elaine nodded. Miriam remained immobile upon the precise spot where they had found her upon entering. When Hyde went on down the hall, Elaine started up the stairs. Miriam followed. When they had reached Elaine's rooms, Miriam questioned:

"Where were you? What on earth prompted you to go off like that without telling anyone where you could be reached?"

"Just a crazy idea, I suppose," Elaine was contrite.

"Was he abominable to you again?"

"No, Miriam; he was very decent."

"Oh." Miriam objected bleakly.

Hyde came up the stairs. Without, probably, being conscious of doing so, Miriam moved away from Elaine, so that they were in opposite corners of the room when he entered.

"Got to run over to see Dad," he informed them. "Tiresome matter of business of some sort. He says I can be back here in time for dinner. Why don't you stay for dinner, Miriam?"

"Thanks, I will if Elaine doesn't mind."

Elaine gave her a sharp glance.

"Well," he said uneasily, "I'll run along then. See you both at dinner. Let's have it at home for a change, or the servants will get all out of practice."

Neither one of them replied to him so he smiled uncertainly and went on out.

Climbing back into the car, he gave George instructions and then leaned back in the seat, thinking deeply.

He asked himself again what strange and shameful method Miriam was using to keep him and Elaine apart. Miriam would not be worried by a scandal in the ordinary sense, but was obviously afraid of being caught at something that would invite the killing scorn and derision of their social set. He thought with morbid pleasure of the power he would hold over her when he found out, the payment he would exact for his silence and protection.

When he had gone, Miriam went close to Elaine.

"So he's been making love to you, and successfully, too!"

Elaine shrugged.

"I thought it was successful, for a while."

"Then you're going to leave him?"

Elaine sat down on the bed, sad and depressed.

"Yes, I guess so."

"Right away?" Miriam brightened.

"No, not right away.... It would seem awfully peculiar ... so soon after our marriage—!"

"Well, what *are* you going to do?"

"Why should it be necessary to leave him at all? The experiment, I'm sure, was as much a failure to him as it was to me. For one thing I'm certain that he wants something I wouldn't give him, if I were sober. He's used to things like that, and since I

can't seem to find any lasting enjoyment in even the more normal manifestations of love, there's hardly any danger that Hyde
and I will have anything in common."

"Do you mean to say that he tried to get you to go in for—"

"No. He didn't."

Miriam had been standing over her like a stern disciplinar-
ian. Now she sat down beside her upon the bed.

"Well, what *did* happen then?"

Elaine explained. Miriam went ghastly white. Trembled.

"You're sure that was all?"

"Yes, that was all. At first, I thought I might learn to enjoy
love like other wives do, but in the last two days—"

Miriam's head lifted a little and she looked exultant. Elaine
went on:

"He'll probably go off now in search of those other things,
and let me alone. What's the difference then if I don't leave him?
If you and I were to go away together you know what it would
be like. The minute we got out of the United States, and traveled
together, without there being men, ever, you know what sophisticated foreigners would say … how they'd look … etc. Why, even
in the United States, now, there are a great many people who'd
thoroughly misunderstand the situation."

"Would you object, terribly, to people thinking, so long as
they didn't actually *do* anything about it?" …

"Yes, I would; I'd feel uncomfortable all of the time and you
would too."

"If you stay will you promise me not to have anything to do
with him?"

"Yes—that's easy to promise. I don't want to and he doesn't—
why concern yourself about it at all?"

Miriam sighed:

"It's just as well that things worked out as they did, Elaine. I feel sure that in another few days his considerateness would have vanished, and he would have reverted to his more natural nature."

She half reclined upon one elbow, beside Elaine. Her perfect hands deftly smoothed a slight crease between Elaine's brows. Softly she remarked:

"You're worried and tense, dear. Did you have luncheon?"

"Yes—before we started out here."

"Want me to go and get you a cup of tea?"

"No, thanks."

"A cocktail then?"

"No, please...."

Elaine shut her eyes. Miriam continued to deftly massage the slight crease between her brows.

"Tell you what I would like," Elaine said.

"What's that, dear?" Miriam questioned, her voice husky.

"I *am* a bit nervous. A good warm bath."

"I'll help you."

Hyde had no intention of going to his father's house. There was no business matter to be discussed and Winton senior had expressed no particular desire to see his son. Hyde just wanted to get out of the house and have a chance to puzzle out the mystery that was plaguing him. He ordered George to drive to the country club, and as the car sped along, he wondered why Miriam was deliberately keeping Elaine from him. He knew that Elaine had been a bit unresponsive physically even before the marriage. He thought hotly of the incident in her bedroom two days before the wedding. And now he sensed from her attitude and remarks that Miriam was industriously entrenching Elaine's frigidity in some morbid but effective way. And the mysterious photographs, that *Miriam* had found! What had they to do with it?

The vague pieces of the puzzle were still tumbling over in his mind as he entered the club. At a table, imbibing a cocktail and a smutty French novel was Rene Mersault. Hyde despised the man. He never smiled, he leered. His snakey eyes lingeringly caressed the form of every woman who entered the room. Hyde mechanically responded to Mersault's invitation to join him, and was almost immediately aware, despite the apparent aimlessness of his remarks, that Mersault had something to tell him, something he considered worthy of interest and lewd speculation. At last, Mersault waxed more intense and inquired slyly.

"I understand that Mees Atwell ees staying with you. Ees she ah ... enjoying 'erself?"

Hyde flushed angrily. How much did this little pig know?

"I hope I am host enough to keep Miss Atwell suitably entertained," he replied coldly.

"Per'aps not, monsieur, per'aps not." His eyes twinkled with delight.

"And what do you mean by that?"

"Eet ees understandable, monsieur. When one 'as a lovely young bride of only a month, eet is difficult to be as charming to one's lady guests as a married man of longair standing. Still, eet seems a shame that a charming young lady like Mees Atwell ees forced to borrow—ah, shall we say "art photographs" from me as her only diversion."

A large portion of the puzzle fell together with startling spontaniety. That was it! Miriam was borrowing lewd photographs from this little leech and telling Elaine that they were his. Elaine, a dainty sex problem that required delicate handling at best, was being deliberately and systematically estranged from him by the cheapest and most contemptible of methods. This was the plot she feared he would discover, the wedge with which she was forcing them apart. He was intensely, savagely happy. The blase members of their set would have been more interested than shocked if Miriam had been merely a "wicked woman," attempting to lure him from Elaine with her body as the conventional bait. But this was far better! This would make her a laughing stock, an object of scorn and derision for all time. He had his hold on her now, for he knew that although the anger of their clique thrilled Miriam like a drug, their amused contempt would be worse than death to her.

Hyde was totally unaware of the creature that sat opposite him, anxiously awaiting his reaction. When none came, Mersault suggested:

"Per'aps I might spend a weekend weeth you soon, and keep the young lady ... ah, amused?"

Wordlessly Hyde stood up and left the room. He had not even heard Mersault's question. He entered his waiting car and said:

"Listen, George; I want you to turn around and drive back home just as fast as you can. When you get back, stop on the trunk road; don't turn in at our private driveway. Let me out there and then drive on up the road. After you've done that, drive back to where our driveway joins the trunk road and wait for me there. Don't blow the horn or anything; just wait there until I come, no matter how long it is. Is that all clear?"

"Yes, sir."

"... And, George ... if there is any talk about my wife's or my affairs, it will get to my father's and mother's servants, and to my wife's parents' servants, and I'll hear of it and somebody will get fired. Good jobs aren't so easy to get nowadays, you know."

"I know that well, sir; I haven't been a private chauffeur for fourteen years without learning to keep my mouth shut. It's the house servants, sir, that talks. The women."

The car turned around and George roared down the trunk road at twice the speed they had been making.

Elatedly Hyde watched the car eat up the remaining mile or so of road back to the house guarded by the stiffly symmetrical trees. It was the only time he could recall when he had approached the house with anything bordering upon pleasure. He grinned to himself as they passed along a stretch of road which had many private driveways, some of them with ornamental gateways, leading off of the trunk road into the private driveways. Now and then he caught a glimpse of magnificent estates, set far back from the road; some of them glazed with the chill of frozen assets and vacant.

There was a stiff, warmish wind blowing in off the ocean which bent the trees along the way. Discovering that he was perspiring he opened one of the car windows. Found himself conjecturing as to whether the stiff, sentinel trees around his house would be bent by the wind, or if they would be motionless, as usual.

Presently the car stopped before his private driveway entrance. Getting out of the car he nodded briefly to George, and started walking up the driveway. There was a graveled road for automobiles, and, on one side of it, a narrow cement sidewalk. Avoiding both the gravel and the cement, he walked upon the ground, just recently denuded of the last snow. It was surprisingly springy soil. It gave him a dizzy, heady feeling. He was thinking of Miriam, white and cold and exquisite. Superb and regal ... forced to gratify his more colorful whims, even as the Sally Tuttles gratified them. How Miriam would hate to do it. How it would humble and sicken her; and yet she'd have to— and the fact that she'd do it unwillingly added greatly to the anticipation.

A chill breath of realization struck him as he became aware, when he neared the house that through him ranted a fever of beastliness that had been entirely lacking until today. What, he wondered, could have come over him?

He noticed the trees. Stopped dead still when he observed that, just as he had expected, they were stiffly erect; silent and still, unbent by the wind. He dismissed the thought almost at once as a childish one. There was some perfectly, natural reason for the wind not blowing here; probably had something to do with the topography of the land which, in all likelihood shunted off the wind when it came from directions not conducive to breeze at this point.

As he approached the house he noted the stillness, and repellent character of it, as he always did. Was, for a moment, reluctant to go in.

Quietly he opened the door with his key. Stepped into the thickly carpeted lower hall. Listened. Apparently there was nobody but the servants downstairs. He could hear them faintly moving around in the back part of the house.

Carefully he mounted the stairs and walked down the hall to the room that led into his suite from the hall. He paused a moment in his room. Heart thumping. Breathing deeply. Trembling.

A reactionary mood came over him. Of course, he assured himself, he was acting like an ass. It was all in his imagination. It couldn't really be possible that—

And then he heard voices in Elaine's suite. Softly he crossed the floor. Cautiously and slowly turned the handle of the door which led into Elaine's suite. Pressed, when he had turned the knob. The door did not yield. It was locked.

He listened; but, though he could hear and identify both Elaine's and Miriam's voices, he could not hear what they were saying.

Feeling decidedly cheap he knelt upon the floor and applied his eye to the keyhole. The key had been turned in the lock, leaving the bottom part of the keyhole free and open. The thing which immediately met his eye was the mirror on Elaine's dressing table.

He could make out Elaine's form, clad in only a translucent black chiffon negligee, sitting on the edge of her bed staring intently at a sheaf of photographs which she held in her lap. Her expression was one of profoundly disgusted fascination. She seemed repulsed and yet stared at each picture with a morbid intensity. Directly in back of her stood Miriam, nude save for a pair of black lace panties, with her thin, hard lips curved in a smile that made her the most terrifying personification of complete evil he had ever seen.

At last he rose; pale, shaken, and, taking a handkerchief from his pocket, wiped the cold perspiration from his forehead.

Weakly he tiptoed back across the floor, down the stairs and into the library. He sat down in a large leather armchair and lighted a cigarette. He knew Miriam's plan and her disgusting method, but what was her object? She had always been after his wealth and position, that much he had known for some time. Now he felt that he possessed something new, something which she wanted with an intensity that bordered on desperation. If he could find out what it was, his power over her would be complete—and then!

An hour later he was still turning up stones in his memory in quest of the missing piece to the puzzle when Miriam walked into the room. Unaware of his presence, she closed the door, and then stood still with the obvious intention of going out again after a moment or so. He heard Elaine giving instructions to the butler in the foyer. Miriam stuffed something in her purse and started to leave.

"Did you want something, Miriam?"

She whirled, startled by his voice and rather surprised to find him there.

"Hyde! Are you back already?"

"It would seem so." Miriam was rarely caught off guard, and it amused him. With no particular object in mind other than a hope that he might discover something new, he remarked,

"I thought Elaine and I might go abroad for a while, to see if we can't work something out."

"The way she feels toward you, what do you think that would accomplish?" She still had the upper hand and well knew it.

"Very probably, nothing at all, but I think it would do us both a great deal of good to get out of this upholstered barn of a house for a while."

He was completely taken aback by the cold rage which took possession of her at this last remark. She glared at him with uncontrollable fury and rage. At last she managed to splutter:

"You repulsive fool! This house is very probably the only thing of beauty you will ever encounter in your dull, shabby life, and you are too stupid to realize it." The same wild look of seething passion was in her eyes as was there when she beat him with the riding crop. She lunged at the doorknob, darted out, and slammed the door with incredible violence.

Hyde was intensely excited. Instinctively he knew that the final piece to the maddening puzzle lay within his grasp. This house! What was there about it that oppressed him? It was more than an atmosphere, it was a living, animate thing, a personality. He was overwhelmed with the sudden, luminous truth of this observation. It was Miriam's personality! But how! With his heart pounding he went to the 'phone and dialed his father's architect.

"Mr. Riordan, please."

"Hello, Mr. Riordan? This is Hyde Winton. Who was the architect who did this house?"

A small, disturbed voice on the other end said,

"Well, Ned Harrison worked out the technical details."

"To hell with the technical details. Who conceived and designed the thing?"

"Well, Mr. Winton, that's supposed to be something of a secret."

"Listen, you want to keep that contract for our Bayonne plant, don't you?"

"Oh, yes sir, please don't misunderstand."

"Then who did it?"

"Miss Atwell, sir, your father gave her a free hand and—"

Hyde hung up the receiver. Memories came winging back to him of Miriam's fanatical devotion to the household duties which Elaine had allowed her to completely usurp. Miriam had conceived and given birth to this house as another woman would a child and now was striving to possess it with a genuine maternal fervor that approached ferocity. It seemed quite plausible that this strange woman, repelled by love in its normal forms, had converted her fierce energies into a maniacal desire to become mistress of her only creation. She was after him because she wanted this house, but what she didn't know was that Hyde's father had put the deed to it in Elaine's name.

"What she doesn't know won't hurt her," he mused with lustful visions of things to come, "or will it?"

# CHAPTER FIFTEEN
## *GOSSIP GETS AROUND*

SUSAN ATWELL, Miriam's mother, was a woman who wallowed in peace with all the whole-souled abandon of a voluptuary wallowing in choice fleshpots.

She had married young. Miriam's father had been a most distressing husband. He had been, apparently, obsessed at all times with the thought that he would die at an early age. His father and his grandfather had died at very early ages. He had seemed always to be trying to pack a long lifetime into a short one by living twice as fast and twice as hectically as a normal man.

He had never done anything in a moderate way. When he was happy he was deliriously so; when he was downhearted he took on all the aspects of a paranoiac suffering from melancholia; and there had been the ever-present migraine which had tortured, baffled and frightened him. He had been afraid of life and afraid of death. He was continually anticipating catastrophes that did not occur: cyclones, earthquakes, floods, fires, explosions. He had never been really sick and never really well. Though he had been dead for years she felt him always near her, ranting around. She inhabited corners; quiet corners and disliked company. Because her daughter reminded her so very much of her dead husband she was never quite at ease with Miriam.

Fortunately her husband had been extravagant in only one particular. Always suspecting himself of having contracted some new ailment he spent thousands upon contemptuous and provoked doctors. But he had neither increased nor diminished the comfortable fortune that his father had left him. The depression, with its glacier-like movement that rolled over all assets and froze them, had considerably diminished her fortune, at least temporarily; but Miriam and she were still comfortably situated.

For a long time she had entertained the hope that her daughter might marry; but at no time had Miriam ever expressed any great interest in men. It had never occurred to Susan to worry about this strange state of affairs. She had struggled, for years, to try to be a good mother to her daughter; though they had, apparently, no interests in common and understood each other not in the least.

Today Mrs. Atwell climbed the stairs to her daughter's room, feeling the necessity for a gesture of motherhood. She hesitated regretfully outside the door, as though she were about to intrude upon a stranger; a baffling, irritating stranger who evidenced the same disquieting nervous energy that her husband had—and he had, in the final analysis, remained, always, during her life, a perplexing stranger to her.

One of the uncomfortable things about dealing with Miriam was that they never met each other's eyes directly. They were always both at great pains not to do so, and always, both, painfully aware of the fact.

Susan felt that her own timidity about meeting her daughter's eyes was due to her secret feeling of guilt over her dislike for the company of her only child. Why Miriam should also feel guilty Mrs. Atwell could not imagine. She knocked timidly. There was an instantaneous and abrupt: "Come in!"

Entering she found Miriam dressed to go out. As always Susan admired her, impersonally, as though she were an impressive stranger. She seemed, in fact, not quite real; not quite possible. She was so sleek and lacquered in her knitted silk frock, with a tiny triangle of red hat showing her shining, dark hair.

"Going out?" Susan asked timidly.

"No. Sit down." Susan sat down, feeling under a compulsion to do so swiftly and jerkily. Miriam always spoke to her thus, exactly as her father had; meaning no unkindness by it. Inevitably, in Miriam's presence Susan felt—exactly as she had felt in her husband's presence—as though she had been suddenly put into one of those crazy motion pictures wherein the movement had been speeded up so that people appeared to dart and dash insanely.

Miriam was by no means ignorant of the fact that her mother did not like to be near her. She had known it from her earliest years, when she had always had one or two nurses, and when her mother and father had been mere "company." ... Her father darting in to pop for a few minutes like a bunch of Chinese small firecrackers, too small to make a wholesome loud noise. Her mother edging in, always feeling out of place. Miriam had the feeling that when she was very young she had with facility read all of the thoughts in all of the minds of those around her. Now she could read her mother's mental attitude toward her with the greatest of ease.

"You feeling all right, dear?" Susan asked, timidly. Miriam sat down in a chair near her mother and offered her a cigarette, as though she were company. Though Susan did not want the cigarette she nervously took it. Miriam held out a lighter. She knew there was something definite on her mother's mind.... Speculated negligently as to what it could be. Often in the past she had longed to put her head upon her mother's shoulder and sob out her troubles; but she had never done so, and now she knew that she would never manage to achieve even a mild basis of familiarity with the woman.

After a long pause Miriam inquired:

"What makes you ask?"

Susan was at once confused.

"Oh, I just thought you weren't looking so well as usual lately.... And I haven't seen much of you in the last few months."

So that was it, Miriam thought. The servants had undoubtedly been talking.

"I've been staying with Elaine and Hyde quite a lot. If you're worried about me when I'm away you can usually get me there."

"How are they getting along?"

"All right, I guess."

"I haven't seen either of them since they were married."

"No, they don't go around much."

"Are they happy together?"

"Seem to be, as far as I can tell."

Susan gave up. Miriam lapsed into silence. She was thinking of a remark Hyde had made at the dinner table the evening before. He had been quoting a writer named Thurston:

" 'Normal people bore me. Being normal is like living in only one room of one's house all of the time. It posits a lack of imagination and enterprise.' "

She recalled the way Hyde had leered at her. Beyond the question of a doubt he knew, now; which was not strange. The only strange thing was that he had not discovered it long before he had. He had known, now, she was sure, for at least a week or so; ever since Elaine and he had come back from that damned five-day honeymoon of theirs. She was beginning to be a bit worn by the suspense of wondering just what he was going to do about it, now that he knew. Certainly he had been as cheerful as ever, and as pleasant toward her; more so in fact. She had rather expected him to insist upon another encounter such as the one in the library which had annoyed her so. But he had not. She could not imagine what was coming. She brought her thoughts back with a snap to the realization that her mother was sitting watching her. Said:

"I suppose the servants are talking."

She waited, but Susan said nothing.

"... Talking about my being there such a lot."

She waited again, but Susan still did not join in.

"... Well, to hell with them, let them talk. If they didn't have *that* to talk about, they'd be chattering about something else; something worse, perhaps."

"It's only," Susan said guardedly, "that I thought you might be worried or unhappy, or something.... I don't care what the servants think or say; or what anybody else thinks or says, for that matter."

Miriam relented a bit; said softly:

"I understand, mother. It was good of you to be concerned. But I can take care of myself."

She knew that her mother was not concerned over the gossip in a social way. Susan cared nothing for society. She asked only to be left alone to exist in quiet corners, and it made no difference to her what people thought of her. Her husband had managed during his life to convince her that *he* was her only *raison d'etre*. After his death it had seemed to Susan that she took on powers of invisibility, having no longer any postulation for her own life.

"I suppose they're saying I'm in love with Hyde, is that it?"

"Something like that," Susan confirmed. "I wouldn't have listened, only I thought perhaps your welfare was involved. You realize, I hope, that even if you were in love with Hyde, and intended to run off with him or something of that sort, I wouldn't condemn anything you did. I'd only want to do whatever I could to keep you from being unhappy."

"Well, I'm not in love with Hyde, and he's not in love with me; and we haven't the faintest intention of running off with each other or anything of the kind."

Miriam had been one of the few children who were able to lie convincingly and logically from the time that they could first talk. Her mother had never caught her in a lie, and had built up an illusion of absolute honesty concerning her.

"I'm glad of that, for your sake, Miriam. Not that I'm old fashioned, as you know ... but it seems to me that only unhappiness usually comes out of those messes."

"You can set your mind completely to rest on that score, mother; I will never, as long as I live, get into a mess like that."

The servants downstairs transferred a call to Miriam's private extension 'phone and rang. She said:

"Pardon me, please," and took up the receiver. Over the wire Hyde said:

"Hello, what you doing?"

"Nothing," she responded guardedly. Elaine, she knew, had gone to visit her mother; she had promised to 'phone before starting home. Miriam had intended to go over to Hyde's and Elaine's place as soon as Elaine started home.

"Come on over and keep me company," he invited. "Elaine just 'phoned that she was going to stay over there for dinner. That means she won't be home for some time after dinner.... Leaves me all alone for dinner and the early part of the evening. We can have dinner together, and then when Elaine comes in perhaps ran into town, all of us, to a night club or something."

"I don't think I'd better," Miriam hedged. There was a slight pause and then Hyde's voice, in an altered tone containing a very decided minatory coloration:

"I *do* think you'd better come, Miriam."

She waited, thinking fast; but she dared not refuse. He knew enough now to completely wreck her plans if he so desired.

"All right," she said dully. "I'll be right over."

# CHAPTER SIXTEEN
## *HYDE GETS THE WHIP HAND*

HYDE WAS in the library when Miriam arrived. He rose as she entered and bowed, she thought, with a slight trace of mockery.

"I'm glad you could come, Miriam. This house gives me the creeps, sometimes; I dislike to stay in it alone, or with these furtive servants who rustle around like rats in dry underbrush."

She sat down without replying. He offered cigarettes and lighted one for her.

"You look charming," he hazarded, a trifle uneasily.

The chauffeur's dog, out behind the house somewhere, howled dismally. Hyde was a trifle aghast at himself; at the vivid impulses which came to life in him; never so much alive as when Miriam was near.

"Suppose," she suggested coolly, "we cut all that and get to the point."

He watched her, somewhat afraid of her, yet desperately intent. It was fascinating to play with her, worry her....

"Elaine will probably be back soon after dinner. She's conceived a dislike for going home and probably won't remain any longer than necessary. It will probably be a half hour or forty-five minutes before dinner is ready."

"Do you mind coming to the point, Hyde?"

"You don't like me—*that way*—do you, Miriam?"

She debated several moments before answering, trying to guess how much he knew.

"No, I don't."

"I'm sorry, Miriam."

"Why?"

"Because I do want you that way."

"Well, you had your way once before."

"Which means, I suppose, that I may have it again if I like?"

"I suppose so."

"But, Miriam, that's not what I want." She saw his scalp slip back and move his hair characteristically.

"What do you want?"

"Come over here and I'll tell you."

She hesitated, then rose and moved uncertainly to where he sat by the library table. He looked up at her for a moment, deliberately leaving her in suspense.

"Sit down on the floor at my feet, and I'll tell you."

Raging inwardly she forced herself to keep outward control. He exulted at the plain antagonism toward his desires that he saw in her eyes now. She did not want to humble herself—to sit at a man's feet. Well, she'd pretty damn well have to. There was, for some reason, great stimulation in realizing that ...

After a momentary hesitation she sat down upon the floor at his feet. Watching her he tried to order his thoughts. There was a mad jumble of desire racing through his mind, tumbling everything else in it into wild disorder. Putting out a hand he touched her hair. It felt just as he had imagined it would, like raw silk. Disarranging a bit of it at her temple he watched the jet black spread over the alabaster white.

He still toyed with her hair; he knew that it maddened her to be caressed that way, and it amused him to worry her. Purposely was dilatory, to prolong the situation. He had instructed the cook to delay dinner.

"... Marriage is a very peculiar thing, Miriam; isn't it? It's curious that so many people have the courage to undertake it at all. How seldom they know how things are going to turn out. Right on their honeymoon they are likely to discover that there is some reason why they could never be happy together.

"I know a girl, a very attractive one, who has never had any real contact with men. She was born and reared up in Maine, by strict parents. She is taking some graduate work at New York University now. She was terrifically attracted to a young instructor down there. She let him kiss her one night. She discovered, when he kissed her, that his nose was oddly cold and slightly dampish, like a dog's nose, though it didn't appear to be any different from the average nose. She thought maybe it was just a temporary thing ... but she let him kiss her again on several occasions. He was a rather backward young man and asked for nothing more. He kissed her over a period of six months whenever he took her to her apartment after they had been out together in the evening. And always she had the same reaction. She would get to liking him again, and the minute she'd feel that cold, wet nose, she'd loathe him. Trifling things like that have enormous significance, as between the sexes; they can mean the difference between a happy marriage and a miserable one. Had she married him, as once she had thought of doing, I am quite certain that she would have been unhappy all of her married life—could never have learned deeply to love and respect him—because, for some reason, she had a particular aversion to cold, wet noses. It might be a thing which traces back into her early youth, before memory started making clear records in her mind. Perhaps when she was a baby she was worried and discomfited by a dog with a cold nose nuzzling her. If that were the case their marriage would have

ended either with her leaving him, or with their being abomina-
bly incompatible.

"Would it be possible now to come to the point?" she
reiterated.

Leaning forward he spoke to her without ambiguity. She
rose, furious, and went toward the door. Opened it. Was about
to pass through and leave him when his sharp voice stopped her
short. She turned slowly and met his diabolical gaze, wondering
if there was anything about her that he did not know. Wordlessly
he arose from his chair and walked toward a window, regarding
her constantly with an air of evil pleasure. He paused, removed a
cigarette from his case, and carelessly ignited his lighter, holding
the small flame perilously close to the rich Burmese drapes as he
did so. His eyes never left her face, and he beheld with intense
delight a look of agonized terror come into her eyes as the drapes
began to smoke and take fire. As she paled and sprang forward,
he extinguished the tiny flame with his fingers and smiled at her
knowingly.

Her heart sank. "You know about the house I see."

"Yes, and I've had a little talk with Rene Mersault too," he
assured her.

Closing the door firmly she locked it. The shades were already
drawn.

"What you demand is out of the question," she asserted
firmly; "you'll have to be satisfied with what you had before—it's
that, or nothing."

He replied in a low, firm tone:

"All right, then, let it be nothing."

She weighed the implied threat in his tone. Considered all
the consequences which might flow out of refusing to gratify his
whim … for that he knew everything now, there was no possible doubt. His tone and manner of speaking conveyed the

information to her indubitably. She could have killed him; considered, in fact, for several moments, the possibility of doing so.

There was a long, tense silence between them. She stood erect and white, one hand resting lightly upon the library table. He stared up at her, not any uncertainty in his eyes; he was calmly waiting. The knowledge of this made her sure that if she had a revolver in her hand she would empty it into him without delay.

… But he held the crop now; there was no escaping that fact. She was completely at bay. There was no way out of the situation.

"This house would be of little use to me without the means to maintain it, Hyde. I think I ought to be able to expect marriage from you after the divorce."

"If you wish it, I promise. It's a matter of complete indifference to me. Now sit down," he ordered firmly.

She moved toward a chair.

"No," he directed; "sit where you were before."

"It's astounding, Hyde, that a man of your rearing could act as you do."

"Nonsense," he contradicted; "it's not remarkable and you know it."

She was surprised that he had not added: "And you should be the last one to question the propriety of a thing like that." Aloud she said: "Suppose I tell Elaine?"

"I wouldn't, if I were you."

She sat where he indicated. She listened dully, thinking only of the trump cards he now held.

When Elaine came in at nine-thirty Hyde was quietly reading in the library. Seeing the light there she went down the hall.

"Hello, honey," he greeted cheerfully. "Miriam's upstairs."

"Oh, is she? I'll run up then if you don't mind."

"Not at all," he replied, without glancing up from his book. "She's not feeling well ... better get her to stay here with you tonight."

Elaine turned and hurried out. Miriam lay limply relaxed upon the bed when Elaine reached her bedroom.

"Migraine?" Elaine asked anxiously. Without opening her eyes Miriam responded:

"No. Must have been something I've eaten. I'll be all right. Just sit down beside me and hold my hand."

# CHAPTER SEVENTEEN
## *MRS. WINTON SHOCKS*
## *HER HUSBAND*

IT IS A deeply significant thing, to which attention is not often enough called, that in all ages and all times the lower classes have believed most firmly in the contemporary god or gods; the middle classes less firmly, and, in the more cultivated civilizations, the upper classes have believed in the contemporary god or gods not at all.

Nevertheless, Mr. and Mrs. Winton, Hyde's parents, went regularly every Sunday to church. They were the apotheosis of the American economic and cultural prototype, De Luxe model.... Family backgrounds tracing clear back to Hudson Bay Trading Posts. A social position so thoroughly unquestioned that they had all but forgotten that they occupied an impregnable social position. An economic background of such impregnable security that even a depression could do no more than put it safely in cold storage for a while. Correctly educated at the right schools; correctly traveled to the right countries, correctly vapid as to all mental activity.

Clad in frock coat and gray striped trousers, Mr. Winton sat stiffly erect in the limousine, after church services; Mrs. Winton, sleekly perfect, sat at his side. She was sixty-five, and looked forty-five. Her husband was eight years her senior. Without his being conscious of the fact he had come greatly to resemble J. P. Morgan, the elder, except for his nose. Without turning to regard her husband Mrs. Winton remarked:

"Don't you think we had better drop in on Hyde and his wife this afternoon?"

"No," he said sharply. "I've got to think about a speech I must deliver tonight."

"But we never see them."

"There is nothing to prevent their calling upon us at any time they wish."

"No," Mrs. Winton agreed; "but they don't."

He lapsed into silence. After a minute she went on:

"I'm not sure everything is going right with them."

"They're restless," Mr. Winton diagnosed. "I had Hyde over the other day and told him that I could manage an European honeymoon now, if he wanted to take one. He had the preposterous effrontery to suggest that they take Miss Miriam Atwell with them. I told him I couldn't afford that extra expense, and he decided not to go."

"Why do you suppose he wished to take her along?"

"I don't know, I'm sure," Mr. Winton observed dryly.

"It's very peculiar," Mrs. Winton said.

"What's very peculiar?"

"Everything."

"I'm sure I haven't the faintest idea what you mean."

"Miss Atwell is over there most of the time. She stays all night."

"Well, she is a very close friend of Elaine's, isn't she."

"Yes."

"Elaine invites her, does she not?"

"I suppose so."

"Well, then, what is there to worry about?"

"I don't know," she replied uneasily. "We wouldn't want any scandal in the family."

"There has never been any. Hyde has been an exemplary son."

"You mean he's never gotten caught yet."

"If you must put it that way, at least if he has been indiscreet at times, he has been considerate enough to keep it from public knowledge. I must say that I am grateful to him for that."

"He might not always be so lucky."

"If you don't mind my saying so I don't think that there is anything to worry about. While I don't, of course, happen to approve of such things, it is a fact that Elaine, Miss Atwell and Hyde are sophisticated young people. I believe they are perfectly capable of handling any situation between them without causing undue—"

"Yes, I know, especially when Elaine is so remarkably complacent. I dropped in to see her the other day. She's upset about something, I can see that. I think it's Hyde, but she doesn't seem to care what he does."

"I suppose she is willing to trust his judgment and good taste, as I am."

"Don't you think he ought to have an occupation of some kind?"

"Yes, indeed; but I'd be afraid of his having anything to do with business right now. Things are in a pretty muddled condition. He might make some costly errors."

"He'll have to take up business some day, will he not?"

"When he is a little older, and conditions in the business world have become more stable, there will be time enough for him to step in. I think you may safely leave matters to me. I feel that I have done pretty well with the boy so far. At least he has passed the most hazardous time in a young man's life splendidly."

"I don't know about that. He's managed to keep things under cover; but you can't tell."

"I'm sure I do not know what you mean; Elizabeth."

"I'm not sure that I do either—but I'm sure of one thing. He's changed enormously since he got married. I feel uneasy when I'm near him; and he doesn't ever look me in the eyes any more."

"I'm afraid you're imagining things."

"No, I'm not. He's entirely different. No matter what he may have done before, at least none of it caused him to lose his own self-respect. Now he's done something of which he doesn't approve himself; of which he's ashamed. He wouldn't feel that way, considering his past experiences, if he were merely flirting with Miriam. It must be worse than that. I can't imagine what it could be to make him feel like that—to make him completely change, so that he isn't his old self at all."

Mr. Winton moved uncomfortably and stared out of the window. He wished that they would reach home so that he could go to his study and prepare his speech. As a matter of fact he didn't care much what Hyde did. He was, himself, above social reproach, in that most of those who might have reproached his family or himself owed him money. So far as he could see, at worst, Hyde might be having an *affaire* with Miss Atwell. He could not bring himself to believe that Hyde—having shown himself to be so careful in the past—would carry the thing to a flagrant condition now that he had arrived at the age of beginning discretion. It was not possible that Hyde would divorce Elaine and go through all of that silliness, merely because he had a temporary fondness for another woman. There would probably, he thought, be a number of other women beyond Miriam; but the thing made scant real difference with Hyde safely married to someone of his own social station:

That a man should actually wish to enjoy the body of a woman to whom he was not married was a thing revolting to him to contemplate; and he did not contemplate it, except in a remote, impersonal way. Still he knew that such things happened. Once, while a senior at Yale, he had almost been seduced by a young actress himself; but somehow or other the thing hadn't gone over. He recalled having thought at the time that to climb into the bed of a socially impossible person would be to lower himself greatly ... there had been no reason, so far as he now could remember, why the young actress should have been deserving of his sexual attentions. True, she had been pretty; but her English had been atrocious and she had probably come of the humblest imaginable stock. Miriam Atwell, however, was quite different. Her family strain, though second rate, was at least conceivable in social terms. She was, perhaps, deserving of the attentions of a Winton, provided the Winton wished to lower himself temporarily.

For years Mrs. Winton had longed profoundly to shock and distress her august husband. At various times she had nearly succeeded in doing so. But she had never quite pricked the shell in which he had, since youth, been safely encased. Now, she felt, she had material which might at last cut through his guard. She launched it without preliminaries:

"What would you say, Josiah, if I were to tell you that I am practically certain that Miriam is using some strange power she has over Elaine to build up a weird sex complex in her that will prevent her ever becoming a normal wife to Hyde?"

After years of effort she had at last succeeded. He turned slowly around to face her. His face was ashen; his eyes large.

"I'd say," he got out at last, "that you ought to wash out your mouth with soap, Elizabeth."

# CHAPTER EIGHTEEN
## *HYDE DATES HIS WIFE*

A LONE IN THE house Hyde tried desperately to think; to apply sheer reason to the whole situation. But thinking, he found, was no easy job to one not habituated to it.

Today he felt entirely different than he had felt for weeks. Something had changed within him, and he had no idea what it could be. Thinking back to the start of it all he recalled that his lecherousness had come on about the time that Miriam had become aware of his intention to marry Elaine.

It was comparatively warm outside. He strolled out of the house without bothering to put on even a top coat.... Remembered that he had never explored the grounds in all the time they had been living there.

"Take an interest in your home, my boy," his father had recently advised, in his best Sunday evening manner. "That's what's wrong with the world today. People don't take enough interest in their homes." His mother had hinted darkly that she knew something was wrong; he supposed that she had urged his father to talk to him. Poor Dad, Hyde reflected in amusement, had never in his life really said anything. If there had been any sort of absolutely protective patent upon the Morgans, *pere et fils,* it would have been impossible for his father to exist at all, since he would have been a walking infringement.

Hands deeply sunk in his trousers pockets Hyde wandered around. Everything, it seemed to him, was rusty and brown. His house appeared to be upon a singularly barren patch of land. Surely Miriam's influence could not have succeeded in blighting the very vegetation around the house she had built, he reasoned. Something about the topography of the section would, he was sure, explain it ... and yet ... perhaps it was a little lower than the adjacent properties. At any rate, on some of the neighboring estates, a few buds had appeared upon the trees; and the brown winter-seared grass had turned a trifle greenish. But not here. Everything was dead and brownish and sere as though no whisper of spring on the way had reached the soil.

The trees gave the impression of being irretrievably dead; but he knew that it was not to mother nature he must look concerning the trees. They were "guaranteed." The poor things had to live, whether or not they were lonesome for whatever soil it was from which they had been boldly uprooted and transported here by the landscape gardener. They were trees, he felt persuaded, that would, if by any means they could, commit suicide.

Walking some little distance away from the house, he viewed it from all sides. He could find nothing greatly wrong with it. But there was, indubitably, about it a sinister air. A suspensive waiting quality. A secretiveness. One unconsciously lowered one's voice upon entering it.

The chauffeur's dog ran out of the garage to greet him. When it approached it lowered its body to the ground, curlike, and crept toward him as though it more than half expected to be struck. Hyde bent down and patted it. Said:

"So you're the beast that howls so eerily at night. What the devil do you howl about? ... But then, I don't blame you."

Thus propitiated the dog sprang to its full stature and raced madly around Hyde in circles, barking, with its tongue hanging out and its ears thrown back. It occurred to him that on another day he would have been more than likely to kick the dog out of his way; today he had petted it. He wondered if the dog noticed that he had changed in some fundamental way.

The dog accompanied him upon his tour of inspection of his own property. The chauffeur was washing one of the cars. He stopped for a minute, watched Hyde to see if the dog were bothering him; decided that it was not, and went on working.

Hyde recalled that it had once been at least an irresolute notion upon his part to become a father. He smiled now, as he confirmed the thought with a feeling of pleasure. Father to a son who would some day also play in the Yale Bowl. He hadn't entertained this notion, he was aware, for days.

That Elaine would be the mother of a prospective son did not enter his mind. Yet he would have been glad could he have thought of her as the mother of a son of his. Against her he held nothing. Had it been by any stretch of imagination possible he would have liked to think of her again in the terms he formerly had. He grew sad at the memory of how once he had contemplated her. If she were vastly different now from what she had been then he could, he realized in all fairness, hardly blame her; for he, too, wast vastly altered. Changed more than she ... except today it seemed all to have been stripped away and he felt again his old self.... Wished that she were around somewhere. There was an excellent tennis court. They might have had a game. He would have liked to see her just as a friend and companion; there was in him no desire for her body, as a body, except as it appertained to her as a person; there was in him today no desire for anything of the fleshly sort. He felt sad, and a little happy too, as though a weight had been lifted from his heart. Sighing, he re-entered the house. Wandered disconsolately around, wondering what on earth to do.

Thurston had introduced him to a most interesting and entertaining chap named Walter Templeton, an artist of no mean ability who staged the sort of pornographic spectacles common in Paris, for the American tourist trade. He decided to go into town and drop in on Templeton; or if Templeton were not at home, or engaged, upon Thurston. Both of them had at least one great thing to recommend them; they were entirely different from anyone else Hyde knew.

As he started out the 'phone rang, and one of the servants, after answering it, called him. Taking up the receiver he heard Elaine's voice:

"Hyde? What you doing?"

It seemed to him that her voice sounded very different than it usually did. He could remember it like that before, but not for some weeks.

"Not a thing. I was wandering around here trying to learn to like the place."

"Miriam's sick."

"Oh, is she?" Hyde felt a peculiar lack of interest in Miriam at the moment.

"Yes. One of her migraine headaches. Probably be ill for several days."

"Do you think that you'll be able to go without seeing any more of those nice pictures for a while?" he asked. His tone was rather bitter, but the bitterness was against Miriam, not Elaine.

'What do you mean?" Elaine's voice was sharp. This was the first time that he had ever hinted to her that he knew. He decided to bait her a bit.

"You know what I mean."

There was a long pause.... Finally her voice weak and frightened.

"Then you know."

"Yes, Elaine."

"What are you going to do?"

"What ought I to do?"

"Well, it's nice of you to take it that way; some men might feel that...."

"It isn't that I don't care for you, Elaine. I was just wondering where you were and wishing you'd call up."

"I've been home. I hate to go there. Of all the questioning and—"

"Yes, I can imagine. I get the same thing at home too. I'm sick and tired of everything ... I wish we could find something different and amusing to do. We've seen all the shows ... there's nothing going on in town that I'm particularly interested in ... except ... you remember that Thurston chap? Well, I met another interesting fellow through him ... a Walter Templeton.... An artist. Paints the damnedest pictures you ever saw; but he's uncommon good at it."

"Yes, I know; Miriam knows him."

"She does—!"

"Oh, she knows a lot of people like that ... writers, artists and poets ... but I never met him. He didn't sound at all interesting."

"But he is, I assure you. Where are you now?"

"I'm calling from the drugstore by the station. Just wanted to see what you were doing."

"Shall I drive over—and take you into town to meet this chap? It might be diverting anyway."

"I've got the limousine. Hadn't I better drive over and pick you and the chauffeur up?"

"All right, come ahead."

When she had hung up he remembered their truancy of approximately a month before. She had talked over the wire in precisely the same mood she'd held then ... what the dev—! Miriam was sick *as she had been then* ... *!* he recalled.

Standing in the hall he reflected deeply; but there was that about the dread stillness of the house which annoyed him. He could not think in it. But he had had, for a moment, a glimmer of something big back in his mind somewhere—it had to do with a thing Elaine had once said in connection with—he could not think what. He must try and remind her. It was all most unpleasant and uncanny ... to completely change for a few days every few weeks and be entirely different. He didn't like it at all. Not that he objected to feeling as he now did; what he vastly objected to was the knowledge that presently he would change back again ... and when he did, the horrible part of it, he remembered, was, that he would prefer *that* state just as, now, he preferred the current one. No wonder, he reflected lugubriously as he went up the stairs, that the chauffeur's dog howled in such a bewitched locality.

# CHAPTER NINETEEN

## *FIVE-DAY PASSION*

LOCKED IN her room, miserable and apprehensive, Miriam stared down out the window.

She saw Max in the yard below. He was working on one of the cars; had taken off its hood. She noticed how broad and strong his back was as he leaned over inspecting the engine while he reached in and revived it by pulling on the accelerator wire.

Max was no fool. Not by the flicker of an eyelash had he betrayed an increase of intimacy between them; so careful had he been in this respect that sometimes she was nearly persuaded that she had only imagined what had passed between them.

She threw herself down wearily and unhappily upon the bed. There was a numbness over her limbs. Her head felt tight. In a matter of hours, she knew, the full force of the attack would be upon her, and her head would feel like bursting.

Debating the thought of using the various sedatives which would ward off part of the attack, she could not bring herself to decide … knowing that though the pain could be thus avoided, the consequent upsetting of the digestion would keep her ill for days afterward.

Restlessly she rose and paced around the room, the dull, dry constriction in her head causing the back of her eyeballs to feel as though they were pressing inward. Stopping before her dressing table she sat down.

Upon the table was an excellent photograph of Elaine. This she studied negligently and numbly. It was strange, she mused, that at the moment she cared not what Elaine might be doing. Didn't care, in fact, if she never saw Hyde, with all his wealth and power, or her beloved house again. She knew that soon the full force of the attack would be upon her, and in the midst of that dull red raging sea of pain, all of it would seem utterly petty and stupid.

She exhaled in nervousness and irritation. Got up again and walked the floor. Sat down upon a small stool before some shelves of books she kept available for those periods when she did not leave the room. One after another she took out volumes and thumbed through them; but none of them held her attention.

She thought with irritation of Hyde and his strange attitude toward her. Had there been any way of doing it, without completely shattering her entire plan, she would have killed him. What, she conjectured dully, would he demand next? ... Not that it mattered; not that anything mattered now, today.

Maybe, she decided, this would be a definitive attack; one of the sort that had taken off her father, and his father before him. Far less afraid of this was she than of the pain which would come during the full force of the attack. With a sigh she got up and threw herself back down miserably upon the bed.

Dressing to go out to dinner with Hyde, Elaine remembered how, the day that Hyde had come to her room at home from the tennis court, after she had called him up, she had felt in herself a vibration similar to the one she had felt in a book she'd carried down Fifth Avenue ... while the heavy vehicular traffic on Fifth Avenue transferred its vibrations to the book in a highly noticeable way.

She felt now as though she had been for days feeling the force and effect of just such a vibration in her own body; and now, abruptly, it had been turned off. She felt a little giddy at its sudden cessation; just as one is made slightly uncomfortable, at first, when a long continued sound of which one had grown unaware, ceases without warning.

Hyde, dressing in his suite, was picturing, with great repugnance at the memory, that first evening with Miriam, in the library.

He recalled with what difficulty he had forced out words. Remembered how he had said:

"You know how it is with music."

... And then, after forcing out that first sentence it had been hard to follow it up ... yet all the time he had known that material with which to follow it had been latent in his mind. Most of the time, lately, he was troubled with a similar disturbance which had at last developed a physiological difficulty that was quite distressing, and from which, tonight, he felt singularly free. He hoped that there would be no return of the symptom.

He had first noticed it about three weeks before. Talking to someone he had suddenly stopped speaking. A constriction had set in somewhere in his throat, so that it seemed for a moment that the muscles which operated his tongue were paralyzed. There had been a frequent recurrence of the phenomenon, so that he had at last become distinctly frightened and worried.

Never in his life bothered by nervous complications it annoyed and irritated him far more than it would have the average man to find himself seized with indubitable indications of nervous disability.

So far as he could reason it out, there was in him somewhere a reluctance to let himself speak with spontaneity, since there was, of late, no telling what the lower depths of his mind might be evolving and shaping toward action, in the form of speech. With this fear in him, the nervousness had grown to the point where his speech was automatically shut off, out of his apprehensions.

Feeling that this might occur, he found himself, when talking fast, and a bit excited, repeating the opening words of a sentence, as though he were beginning to stammer. The thought of becoming a stammerer so frightened him that fuel was added to the nervous strain, and the thing grew steadily worse.... But tonight, for some reason, it was all gone, and he felt no traces of nervousness.

Finished with his dressing he opened the door and went into Elaine's suite. She was clad in dainty lace edged panties and a brassiere. She turned to speak to him over her shoulder:

"I'm sorry, Hyde. I *am* slow, aren't I."

"No hurry, Elaine. Take your time. I like to watch you dress."

He sat down and crossed his legs. He was aware that he keenly anticipated the evening with her. After several moments, while he watched her powdering her shoulders he asked:

"Why don't you have the maid assist you with those things?"

She made a wry face:

"I can't stand her."

"What's wrong with her?"

"Nothing that I could charge her with."

"Why don't you get another one?"

"It wouldn't be a bit of use. A new one would get to be like the old one after she'd been around here a week. I don't know what it is, but this place certainly does ruin servants."

"Yes, I know. But I suppose Dad would think I was mad if I suggested taking another place so soon. We can at least stay away from it as often as we like. And, when you come right down to it, it's probably not the place at all; it's just us. God, Elaine, why can't we be as we are now all of the time? I don't give a damn about our sex life. If you can't find pleasure in any other way than indulging in visual pornographic orgies, it's quite all right with me; I have my notions, along those lines too; but there are periods when we are such great pals, despite everything—just as we used to be. Sometimes I'm sorry that I ever proposed to you."

She turned toward him.

"Yes, I've thought of that."

"Do you suppose, Elaine, it might be better if we were divorced? ... In, say, six months or so."

She considered for a moment. Said, at last, honestly:

"It's peculiar, Hyde ... that ... ordinarily I'd say yes, but tonight.... It may sound ridiculous to say it, Hyde, but I *do* care for you a lot."

"I know you do. *For Lord's sake!*" he burst out; "what ails us anyway? What's wrong? Have we both lost our minds?" When she made no comment he continued:

"*Other* married people who get along perfectly happily are often situated much as we are. I know other wives who can't stand physical contact with their husbands, and yet are strongly attracted to the subject. Their husbands have endless *affaires,* extra-marital, and they get along all right. What's the matter with us? I'd love to have you as a comrade ... I'd like to be on the old basis with you—and I can only be so about once in six weeks. A change comes over me. I can't explain it coherently."

"It's probably my fault, Hyde. I change. I can feel myself change, greatly, at times; but I don't seem to be able to help it at all."

He got up and went over to her side. Leaned down and kissed her. Said, softly:

"There are times, Elaine, when I love you desperately and want to somehow reach you, and can't."

She patted his hand.

"I know. I feel that way too. I even feel that it might be possible for us to love a very great lot—to have something between us that would mean all the brightnesses my dear old grandmother used to talk about—and yet I can't escape from—Oh, I don't know what. I've an idea. But it's an utterly mad one.... Better let me finish dressing, dear; let's get to hell out of this accursed place. I'd still like to burn it up."

"Me too," he confessed morosely, and started pacing the floor. But for something—something which was not solid enough to be dealt with in a forthright way—he knew that they could have been greatly happy together; and he was sure, too, that the something would always operate. Vastly unhappy he continued to pace until she announced herself ready to go. And then he brightened.

"Well, anyway, we'll be happy together for a few days, and then—"

"Yes, about five days," she concurred thoughtfully; "and then I'll change again."

"Five days!" he echoed.

"I'm going to watch carefully this time, Hyde. If it *is* five days, if it ends when—but then even if that *is* it I don't know what I'll do, because I'll change completely again then and won't even *want* to solve—"

"I don't follow you at all, Elaine. I don't know what you mean."

"I'm not sure that I do either; but I think I will be sure this time when—come on, let's forget everything tonight, and after we've run around 'till we're tired go and play hookey again in your little hideout."

"Splendid!" he agreed, grinning with his old boyish exuberance.

# CHAPTER TWENTY
## *RENDEZVOUS WITH MIRIAM*

T HERE WAS a ring on the bell which had its button in the hallway. Hurrying to the door Hyde opened it. Miriam walked
slowly in, erect and angry.

"Well," she inquired, "may I ask why you had the effrontery
to order me to come down here?"

"Sit down," he directed. She sat down upon the divan without
taking off her hat. He offered her a cigarette which she absent-
mindedly took. Lighting it for her he seated himself opposite.
It was mid-afternoon, and somewhere closely overhead a group
of airplanes were maneuvering. They sounded like Gargantuan
wasps bent on vengeance. From where he sat Hyde could see
out of the window, down into the valley below, because of the
eminence upon which the apartment building was placed; the
highest point of ground in New York City. The sun was behind
the building so that he could not see it; but its sharply yellow rays
colored the ugly valley below in startling fashion, bringing some
manner of beauty to the hundreds of square blocks of ugly buildings, with the elevated weaving through them like a geometrical
snake. Thousands of the windows in the buildings became bril-
liants and blazed with yellow light as they reflected the sun. The
row after row of dilapidated structures faded into the horizon in
jagged fashion, cutting into its edge like a rusty saw.

"You once said," he reminded, "that you would like to see the place where Elaine and I go 'A. W. O. L.' This is it. I call it my hideout."

She surveyed the room incuriously.

"I don't know why you should need a 'hideout,'" she observed, not at all cordially.

"Oh, I rather think you do," he contradicted; amused, as usual by her unwillingness to be with him, and by her fear to refuse to do whatever he asked.

"Are you completely recovered now, Little Witch?"

"Did you say 'witch?'"

"Yes, Witch. For you are a witch, you know." He said it wholly humorously; but he saw her eyes dilate. "When you are indisposed, Elaine and I are freed of your spells. The moment you recover, a change comes over us. I can't speak for what happens to Elaine; but I can speak for what happens to myself: I change from a not extraordinarily wicked young man into an appalling sort of fellow. And I'm afraid you'll have to pay for what you do in bewitching me." Though he had been smiling as he spoke she did not rally to his mood. She appeared solemnly to be digesting what he had said. Presently she remarked:

"Of course you know that's all damned nonsense."

"Yes, of course, I do. Still...."

For several moments neither spoke.

He recalled how she had looked that night when she advanced upon him with Elaine's riding crop, eyes blazing. Passion ranted through him. She had hurt him. She was interfering with Elaine's and his happiness. He would punish her, and at the same time treat himself to—she interrupted his thoughts with:

"Well...

His eyes swept over her.... Tempting and dainty. His to do with as he liked. Inwardly she debated the feasibility of this time refusing him. But she dared not. His influence over Elaine was growing. And the gossip out on Long Island was raging ... at last people seemed to be on the right scent. One word from him and her whole world would crash down around her. Her mother and she would have to leave their home. They did not have the means to go abroad, or to establish themselves in another wealthy community once they lost what they had here. It would mean losing all chance of ever becoming mistress of Winton Hall. Not yet, she decided, did she dare cross him. So long as Hyde said nothing, made no motion, the others would not; they would gossip, but they would only half believe their own innuendoes so long as Hyde remained outwardly her friend. He, alone, held the key to the whole situation; he could make or break her in every direction. Awareness of this she saw now reflected in his eyes. She longed to kill him; yet she knew that she must not. Wearily, her voice hardly audible, she asked:

"*Now* what do you want?"

He was explicit. Again she longed to slay him.

"Is it your intention to humiliate and torture me to the point where I shall have to resort to suicide for escape from you?"

"You won't do anything like that, my dear, so long as Winton Hall stands.... But why look at the thing that way at all? Why not look at it constructively? It's un-American, you know, not to put some sort of constructive angle on everything.

"... Think what a good sport I have been, Miriam. Do I ever interfere with your scheme? Don't I even go to some lengths to make opportunities for you? Isn't it a fact that I protect you at every turn? Without me that pack of snobs we call our friends would pick your pretty corpse apart like a pack of vultures, and that damned house could never be yours."

"The hell of it is," she remarked dryly, "there's sufficient of truth in what you say to make it uncomfortably plausible. But how much longer is this thing going to continue; how much farther—"

"It can't go any farther, Miriam; this is the end of passionate possibilities as between one man and one woman.... And it couldn't very well go on much longer anyway, because one grows tired of even the most delectable dainties, unless there is an ingredient added to passion to sustain interest ... and I assure you, my dear, that I shall never fall in love with you."

"... Well, my dear, Hyde, for *that,* at least, I can be thankful.... But when you get tired of this, what then? When you no longer want me, how do I know that you'll marry me and keep your end of the bargain?"

You ought to know me better than that, Miriam."

"Yes ... I think I can trust you in that direction.... And it's peculiar, Hyde, that I *do* feel that I can. I've never known anyone lower and meaner than you have become since you married Elaine."

"... Nor I," he concurred sadly. "I don't know what's come over me. I'd like to have the strength of will now to say: Forget it all, Miriam; go on and break up this cursed marriage, it's what Elaine and I both want anyway. Have your gaudy parties and make all those tin gods crawl to you, it's little enough to ask of life.

"... But I'm sorry, Miriam, I can't say it ... or take that attitude."

"Why can't you?"

"It's hard to explain. Perhaps I ought to have lived in the time of Petronius, when it was fashionable to be as I am now. I can't help it. I'm deuced sorry.... Really, I am."

A cold breath of dark fancy blew over her. For a moment she was nearly persuaded that she did have an occult influence over him, and over Elaine.... Or perhaps, she thought, it was that *she* was in some strange way possessed, and the bewitch-ment passed through her conductivity to her friends.

But all this, she inwardly counseled, was absurd. Aloud she said:

"... All right, let's get it over with."

His scalp slipped bade, taking his hair with it for a fraction of an inch. She investigated the other room.... Went in and closed the door. Soon he heard the shower being operated. He paced the living-room floor in great agitation.

One part of his nature censured him severely; while another part—perhaps that part which was age-old and refused to accept the mewling limitations put upon passion by the milk and water gentlemen of the Twentieth Century, all of whom would have seemed like anaemic lilies to the rumbustious gentlemen of the first recorded centuries—urged him on.

After a time he heard her call from the next room. He entered. Smooth, warm whiteness greeted his eyes. The tips of his fingers prickled with tiny pains like the fleeting touch of hot needles. His scalp itched.

# CHAPTER TWENTY-ONE
## *DOES EVERYBODY KNOW?*

O F THE POMPOUS, Morganesque Mr. Winton, Wesley Vanner had long stood a bit in awe. Not that he revered or admired him; nor was he really afraid of him. Rather it was that he viewed him as a spectacle, a remarkable spectacle, the like of which there was not another such extant.

Josiah Winton would have been distinctly flattered had he known that Wesley Vanner considered him a greater show than the living Morgan. The living Morgan, Wesley Vanner slightly knew. He knew, for instance, that the current Morgan was capable, under certain circumstances, of evidencing human traits which proved him mortal. But Josiah Winton, so far as Wesley Vanner knew, had, never evidenced the slightest tendency toward the estate of reality as a human being. It was possible, for instance, to visualize the dead J. P. Morgan standing before his mirror in his bathroom gingerly feeling of his proboscis, which had sprouted so amazingly toward the end of his life, and making wry faces into the mirror over the spectacle. But it was sheerly impossible to visualize Josiah Winton so much as fiddling with a particularly tempting pimple.

He was always at a loss to know what on earth to talk about when he was alone with Winton. Actually he was grateful to the man, though he well enough knew that the loans he had received from him, which assured a comfortable old age, had been merely posited upon the marital arrangement as between their families. It had been worth a lot to Josiah to see Hyde actually married to a girl whose social position was right, and whose economic position could be assured without too much cost.

Amy, he knew, was suffering too; she was in the living room talking to Mrs. Winton. Mrs. Winton preserved the ridiculous formality of rising from the dinner table to "leave the men to their cigars" after dinner. Wesley felt a wild impulse in himself to ask Josiah if he had seen "The Three Little Pigs." He fell to speculating hysterically as to what Josiah Winton's reply might be should he be so rash as to propound such a query. Josiah cut in on his reflections, after a silence that had lasted fully three minutes, with:

"Wesley, what's the matter with Elaine and Hyde?" Wesley was startled, he echoed vaguely:

" 'Matter with them?' "

Josiah squirmed around in his seat and puffed at his cigar.

"Dislike to bring up such a subject. Hate gossip. Never listen to it. But Elizabeth says that our servants ... your servants, and, confound it, Elaine's and Hyde's servants...."

"I'd like to fire the lot of them," Vanner cut in with asperity; "but it's so darned hard to train new ones."

"You've heard things too, then, Wesley?"

"Yes. Amy's reported...."

"What do you make of it?"

Vanner considered. How was it possible to discuss such a thing, he wondered, with the imitation Morgan across the table from him.

"There's Miriam Atwell mixed up in it somewhere, I've been informed," Vanner got out uneasily.

"Hrrrrrmmmm! Yes!" the other agreed. He twisted again in his chair and appeared to be decidedly uncomfortable. He had remembered his wife's conjectures. Even to think of such a thing pained him so inexpressibly that he ached.

"Elizabeth dropped in on Miriam's mother the other day. They had a talk. Nothing came of it. Elizabeth said, however, that Mrs. Atwell appeared to be worried about Miriam. The girl, I am informed, is subject to an ailment bordering upon epilepsy—"

"Perhaps," Wesley contributed meekly, "but is that any justification for the manner in which she seems to be trying to warp Elaine?"

"What is the world coming to, Wesley?" Not knowing, Wesley hesitated to reply.

"Strange things do happen," he contributed meekly.

"Have you spoken to Elaine, Wesley?"

"I! Speak to my daughter on such a subject?"

Winton looked annoyed. Whenever he said or did a stupid thing it was his habit to look vastly annoyed at whomever happened to be near and thus indict them for his own stupidities.

"Amy has spoken to her," Wesley offered.

"I've spoken to Hyde again about going to Europe for a time," Winton went on. "I think he's willing to go, just Elaine and he, now. Once he wanted to take the Atwell girl with them."

"The hell he did!" Wesley was startled. He knew that Winton loathed profanity; but though in awe of the man, and indebted to him, he did not truckle.

Josiah, however, was not so much upset by an expletive this time as he usually was. He had been so profoundly moved by a reluctant realization of the situation between Hyde, Miriam and Elaine, that nothing much could shock him any more. He was almost affable:

"You know, Wesley, I'm glad I've only got one son."

"I know," Vanner nodded... And I'm glad that I've only got one daughter. Bringing up young folks nowadays is certainly a problem.... But I rather think everything's going to be all right between Elaine and Hyde. No matter what happens, we've got to give the young folks in this generation credit for one thing.... No matter what they get into they seem to be able—most of them—to get out of it without slopping over too much."

"Yes," Winton nodded. "But things have certainly come to a pretty pass, when parents have to worry because their daughter *won't* sleep with a man when she is finally married after spending half a lifetime worrying that she *will* sleep with one when she's not."

Wesley laughed outright; and then sobered. Watching Winton's face he was disconcerted to find that the man had not the faintest conception that he had given voice to something almost approaching a witticism.

"Don't you feel, even so, a bit anxious about Elaine?" Winton asked severely.

"Yes, I do," Wesley confessed; "but she has poise. She's pretty well balanced. I look at it this way, Josiah: Just think of all the things she *might* have gotten into these last few years and *didn't.*"

Winton nodded in accord.

"You're right, Wesley. You're right. That's why I'm willing to forgive Hyde a lot. He's done pretty well too."

Josiah heaved a sigh of relief and turned to other topics.

In the large living room Amy also was having rather heavy going. Elizabeth was the prying sort. She had, during the past half hour, prefaced not less than twenty outrageous remarks with: "But what do you suppose they...."

Desperately Amy endeavored to change the subject; but Mrs. Winton was all for nursing it.

"I got some books," she informed Amy. "But I couldn't read them. They dealt with the subject …"

Speaking of books, Elizabeth, have you seen the latest Book Club selection, 'Gestured Gethsemanes?' "

"Yes, I've got it somewhere at home. Somehow or other I never get time to read them; but I'm going to catch up some day—I'm keeping them all carefully…. You know, it's a terribly delicate matter of course, but I can't help but think we've got to *do* something about it."

"About 'Gestured Gethsemanes?' "

"No, no; about Miriam Atwell."

"Poor Miriam," Amy sighed. "At first I felt a little that way too; but now that I come to think it over … the poor child … she has no one and she is such a loveless creature herself that perhaps she feels it her duty to keep Elaine from Hyde *that* way. Of course she is not normal.…"

"Of course she's not."

"… So I don't suppose she can help matters much, can she, Elizabeth?"

"Help not being normal you mean?"

"Yes."

"Well, no, I suppose nobody can help not being normal. But that's hardly any excuse for—"

"Of course if we knew, if we had evidence.…"

"Hasn't Elaine said a *word* to you?"

"No."

"And you've questioned her?"

"Well, not directly, of course, how could I question her directly about a thing like that? I'd simply die of embarrassment."

"Yes, I know," Elizabeth nodded regretfully. "But it's *too* humiliating … practically *everybody* knowing. What are we going to *do?*"

"I'm afraid there isn't much we can do, except trust to the thing wearing itself out as, I suppose, it ultimately will. I wish they would go abroad this summer, Elizabeth."

"That's it. That's just it, Amy. If they only would. If Hyde and she would just go away, for six months. Then maybe the whole thing would stop."

"Yes, that would be nice. I've urged Elaine to go but—"

"I know. Josiah has spoken to Hyde too, but he won't go either. Hyde's attitude toward it is what puzzles me more than anything else."

"Hyde's a thoroughly good sport, Elizabeth."

"Yes. I suppose one could call it good sportsmanship. At least thank Heaven he's got sense enough to cover things up, if that's good sportsmanship."

"Have you seen the psychiatric clinic since it was dedicated, Elizabeth?"

" 'Psychiatric clinic?' What psychiatric clinic?"

Amy laughed.

"My dear you are *distraught*. You were the chief patroness for the clinic you know ... the one for working girls."

"Oh, yes! No. I haven't seen it; it's in such a messy neighborhood. Do you suppose if *I* were to talk to Elaine?"

"You might try, Elizabeth; but she's totally evasive on the subject.... Miriam and she were friends long before the marriage, you know, and naturally it will be difficult for her to understand that Miriam would tell her anything that was not for her own good."

"It's beyond me, Amy. I wish I could keep from worrying about it as you do."

"Oh, I worry about it, Elizabeth; but not so much as I did at first. At least one thing I'm sure of. Hyde and Elaine will manage it somehow without complications."

"But the talk that's going around now!"

"Yes, I know," Amy sighed. "But you know how it is out here on Long Island. If it isn't one thing it's another. In former years I've been named as the shameless woman in at least twenty imaginary *affaires,* and never once did they name the right man."

"The right man, did you say, Amy?"

"I mean never once was there anything in it.... And practically everyone I know on this part of Long Island, who's been here as long as we have, has been gossiped about at one time or another; yet whenever a *real* scandal breaks, you find out nobody even dreamed of suspecting the principals beforehand."

"I know," Elizabeth nodded. "Even I have been talked about." She hadn't been; but she could not bring herself to admit it. "... And you're right—the real *affaires* are always a surprise; it's only the ones that didn't happen, usually, that get attention from the scandalmongers."

"That's another reason why I don't worry about this present situation, Elizabeth. I think all those who are so busy talking about Elaine and Hyde and Miriam now sort of half suspect that there really isn't anything in what they're saying."

"That's a comforting thought," Mrs. Winton agreed, somewhat mollified.

"You going to the bridge luncheon at the Merediths Thursday, Elizabeth?"

"I suppose so."

"I think I'll accept."

The clock in the hall chimed. Elizabeth jumped up:

"I *must* be running along, Amy; it's been lovely being here.... But Josiah will be cross if we don't get started now."

"Oh I do wish you wouldn't go," Amy begged, hoping that she would hurry and go and never come back again.

"Oh but I *must,* dear. Josiah is so tired in the morning if he doesn't get to bed by nine-thirty at least. And you mustn't wait so long before coming to see us again." Privately Elizabeth hoped that Amy would never come near her again so long as she lived, since she couldn't or wouldn't share the details of a juicy situation when at last she had stumbled into one.

Elizabeth routed Josiah out of the dining room.

"Oh don't go," Wesley begged, grateful to the bottom of his heart to get rid of both of the pests.

After they had gone he turned to Amy when the servants were out of earshot:

"Well, thank God *that's* over; they won't visit us for another six months now, I hope."

Amy yawned widely:

"God, I'm bored to death. What that woman needs more than anything else is a set of pornographic Parisian photographs."

They went upstairs together, crushed by the weight of the imitation Morgan and his unspeakable wife. Amy was picturing them to herself, going home in their car. At the present moment Elizabeth would be leaning toward her husband intently and pouring out a garbled "And then she said! and then I said," recital of everything that had passed between them during the evening, and much that had not.

# CHAPTER TWENTY-TWO
## *ELAINE'S SECRET*

ALL OF THE way along the trunk road toward town Hyde held, amusingly, the memory of Miriam coming in just as he had left the house.

He felt in a particularly gay mood.... One of those irresponsible moods which came often upon him of late, predicated partly upon a sense of desperation which threw off all concern for matters other than finite and temporal ones.

It was a bright, warmish day, and the sing of the car's vacuum cup tires upon the perfect cement highway was pleasant to hear. He had in mind going to Thurston's when he reached town; perhaps Thurston and he would go to Walter Templeton's—anything to break the general monotony of living. Somehow, foolishly enough, he remembered, he had supposed that marriage would in some esoteric manner change everything; make everything different—whereas, of course, nothing was in the least different, and he was put to the same old necessity of spending most of his time inventing ways and means to dispel the great enemy of all "fortunately" situated young men—boredom.

He recalled how, shortly before the marriage, he had viewed the possibility of divorce with intense alarm, and in naive terms. He chuckled cynically to himself and then sobered.

Love ... he speculated. What in hell was it; where did it come from; how did it get started, and when did it stop?

He had, he was aware, formerly thought of it as a sort of malady that one caught, like measles. At least he had learned differently about that.

　… It was, in short, a thing one made oneself; with one's own hands and brains and great efforts. Easy enough now it was to see that when a man and a woman married they might be drawn together by any one of several things…. Propinquity…. Social fitness…. Sex appeal. Expedience…. Perhaps, even, just because marriage was a new diversion when there was nothing else to do.

　If they subsequently began to love each other, he now saw clearly, it would be because one or both of them built up the loving, carefully, painstakingly and devotedly.

　… If they divorced it would be because, all along—whether they both believed it or not—one or both of them had not been making anything out of their association…. Had been shirking the job of building.

　If one of them had been building up love, that one would surely fight divorce. If both of them had, day by day, been building up love between them, there would never be any divorce. People never tore to pieces things that they had themselves made with their own hands and hearts and souls.

　… Sheer laziness, he was inclined to believe, was to be held accountable for more divorces than was infidelity, incompatability, or total unsuitableness. Not many couples, he was sure, had between them such flagrant causes for divorce as there were between Elaine and himself.

　… And that their association must eventually end in divorce he now saw quite clearly…. Sighed. After all—if things had been different he felt that he would have been very glad—but there was no hope. No likelihood was there, surely, of Elaine ever overcoming what ailed her; and no likelihood was there of his ever overcoming what ailed him; in fact he realized, he didn't even *want* to overcome it—except at those strange, rare intervals when his mind was in some mysterious way freed of its obsessions, as was Elaine's, at the same time.

... Yes, he sighed to himself, it would, inevitably, end in divorce; one might as well face the thought and be done with it. As for marrying Miriam, he might as well. It was a fair deal, he thought with a bitter smile, each of us has what the other wants.

But the day was too fine, and his spirits too high long to maintain a lugubrious mood. He chuckled again at the memory of Miriam entering just as he left ... the odd glance she had vouchsafed him ... the amused grin he had given her. On impulse he leaned forward:

"Turn back home, George," he called, and his scalp moved and prickled.

When the car had turned around he leaned back comfortably upon his seat and sat with a fixed grin staring out at the landscape.

After all, he thought, what the devil would they do about it? He held the whip hand. He could do as he liked, and neither one of them could object. Why should he have any compunctions? ... On second thought he was aware that there were many reasons why he should have compunctions, not the least of which was the bad sportsmanship involved; but somehow the thought did not deter him, as it would have formerly; or as it still might at those rare intervals when, for a time, he found himself restored to his normal estate of manhood.

"Put the car in the garage," he instructed George, when they reached home. "Take it easy; if I want you again I'll call you ... but I don't think I will for a long time."

Entering he went upstairs. Walked through his rooms to the door of his wife's suite. It was slightly ajar. He had supposed that they would have heard the car crepitating upon the gravel private roadway; but evidently they had not. He pushed the door open boldly.

The two girls lay on the floor clad in filmy nightdress that rendered them more enticing than complete nudity. Before them on the floor lay five or six large glossy photographs of the most lewd and sensuous variety. They leaped to their feet, startled and amazed.

"Hyde!" It was Elaine. "It's not like you to do a thing like this."

"It's like him to do anything!" Miriam ejaculated, and then in a rush, she informed Elaine of Hyde's other malfeasances. When she had finished her somewhat lengthy recital Hyde grinningly confessed:

"It's all quite true, Elaine."

Elaine said nothing. She stared helplessly from Miriam to Hyde. Miriam turned and strode toward the riding crop still hung upon the wall.

"Better be careful," Hyde counseled. But, not heeding, she snatched the crop from the wall and approached him.

"I was half drunk, weak and helpless that other time you know, my dear," he reminded her warningly. She struck out at his face with all her strength. Catching the crop in his hand he jerked it from her. Before she could regain poise he grasped one of her slim wrists; twisted it sharply; with a little cry she sank to the floor.... Lightly, but with sufficient emphasis to sting but not injure he applied the crop where it would meet the safest and most easily reached surface. She squirmed and struggled; cried out in pain; but he did not desist.

Elaine sprang across the room and jerked the crop from him.

"Have you gone insane, Hyde?"

"Nope," he said. "Just returning, in very small measure, the lacing Miriam once gave me. If she will just rub some cold cream on the place where she's injured she'll be all right."

Elaine stood rooted to the spot, holding the crop; too distraught to know what to do.

There was a knock on the door. Elaine, Miriam and Hyde exchanged glances uneasily. Elaine called out:

"Who's there?"

"It's me, Mum," came the voice of the housekeeper. "I thought I heard someone cry out."

"That was I," Elaine lied. "I pinched my finger. It's all right. Go away. I'll call you if I need you."

The servant moved off. The two women stood close together, both turning startled eyes upon Hyde; Elaine terrified, Miriam raging and defiant.

"Don't worry," Hyde smiled. "Everything's going to be all right." A hell of passion was raging in him at the sight of so much female loveliness. "I've no objection to your little cult, my dears; in fact, I think it's rather nice, but two's company; three's a carnival, as Aretino might have said."

"Hyde! You ought to be *ashamed!*" Elaine objected, turning away. "What's gotten into you?"

"Nothing.... I guess it was always there. I must have been born with it there. I'm sure it's in all men.... What's happened is that something's let it out of me...." It was obvious that Elaine was overcome with shame. Miriam was furious.

"You filthy beast," she hissed. He moved toward her. She retreated timidly. He did not pursue, but spoke in a placating manner:

"Sorry, Miriam, to butt in like this ... but you must admit that I've been a good sport throughout everything. I've never interfered before, and I'm not going to spoil your game now."

"Well then why the hell don't you get out of here?" Miriam wanted to know. She tried to make her voice sound firm and threatening; but despite her will there was an edge of fright on it. Without their French heels both Elaine and she appeared diminutive and childlike before Hyde who towered over them.

"Listen," he begged, in a conciliatory tone; "you needn't be afraid. There isn't going to be any scandal, or anything like that. I'll go, in just a short while, and then you two can have the whole art gallery to yourselves. I'm not coming back tonight. Perhaps I won't return for several days. I haven't the faintest idea of making things tough."

"You've made it tough enough for me already," Miriam accused. "You said there wasn't any more; you said that—"

"I know I did," he agreed. "... Only; well—it's up to Elaine. If you two want to string on with things as they are it's all right with me.... And I won't bother either one of you any more after today ... but it occurred to me that Elaine is probably weary of looking at mere pictures and would enjoy a real live show." Hyde's regard met Miriam's furious gaze.

"Make him go," Miriam implored of Elaine. Elaine glanced imploringly at Hyde. He smiled at her so friendlily that she relaxed and sat down on the bed.

"Why don't you go, Hyde?" she asked, calmly enough now.

"Because I've got an idea."

"You've got too damned many ideas," Miriam all but screeched at him.

"Careful, Miriam!" Elaine implored. "The servants."

There was silence for a minute. Miriam backed away and sat down, then jumped up. Grinningly Hyde tossed her a cushion. Placing it in the chair she seated herself with a dignity which was so ludicrous that both Hyde and Elaine smiled. Even Miriam was forced a trifle to relent.

There was no talk between them for several moments. Miriam and Elaine exchanged glances. Elaine plainly implored Miriam to be indulgent.

Hyde grinned sardonically.

# CHAPTER TWENTY-THREE
## *MIRIAM'S PREMONITION*

T SEEMS that the most portentous revelations fall from the lips of those who have no knowledge of the gravity of their words. It happened one day as Miriam and Elaine were on their way to an art gallery. As the limousine wound its way through the tortuous streets of Greenwich Village, Elaine breathed a great sigh of relief and said,

"It's so good to get out of that house. You know, it's the first thing I've ever completely owned in my own name, and yet ..."

"*You* own it?" Miriam exclaimed in great dismay.

Elaine was surprised at this strange outburst. "Why, yes, Hyde's father had the house and the property put in my name after we were married as a wedding present. Why do you ask?"

Miriam controlled herself with great difficulty, "Why ... I don't know, I just supposed that ... I guess I never pictured Mr. Winton giving anything to anybody but Hyde."

Inwardly, she and her dream were crumbling like a sand castle in the tide. Hyde; the low dog! She had humiliated herself for him, gratified his wildest whims, had gained control of him as completely as he had her ... for nothing! For some time now, Elaine had been slipping away from her and she had not considered it important. Hyde was the important one, she had thought. And now, when success was in her grasp, it meant nothing! What a fool she had been, not to make sure that the house was Hyde's. She remembered clearly now that he had promised her marriage, but never Winton Hall. An overwhelming sense of the utter futility of it all engulfed her like a shroud. Her head throbbed with the first evidences of a severe oncoming attack.

It was like old times Elaine thought; this "exploring" with Miriam ... who was always finding new and interesting things to do.

They alighted before a house on Eighth Street and entering found themselves not in a dwelling but in a museum. Before them, by the side of a stairway, was a bust made of what appeared to be ebony. The head was grotesquely elongated, and the shoulders were abnormally narrow; yet the thing did have a queer impressionistic effect that was striking.

They wandered around the main floor viewing other bits of sculpture and paintings, all of them warped and twisted in some way; all of them crying aloud of warpedness and twistedness on the part of their creators a warpedness and a twistedness that went just a bit beyond that latent in the average person's mind.

They went upstairs. There were more of the grotesque paintings and sculptured figures. Miriam asked:

"What do you think of it?"

"Interesting, Miriam.... A person who wasn't normal would feel comfortable in here ... one who was would be frightened and uneasy."

Miriam laughed. "And how do *you* feel, my dear?"

"... Just interested."

Miriam felt a tinge of rebuff in the reply; felt that Elaine had subtly mocked her. She drew a little away from her.

Elaine stopped before the picture of an acrobat in white tights. Miriam came over and viewed the picture. Uttered an exclamation of impatience.

"Some of these things are disgusting, aren't they, Elaine?"

"They all are a little bit that way," Elaine confirmed. "It is as though the one-armed men of the world got together and declared that no picture of a human being was worth anything unless it had only one arm. These artists have various mental deficiencies ... and they express them in their work defiantly, with somewhat the same feeling that one-armed men probably have that two-armed people are noxious."

"They have a right to substantiate themselves," Miriam defended.

"Beyond a doubt," Elaine agreed; "but an art museum for one-armed people would, logically, be of interest only to one-armed people.

They climbed another flight of stairs. The top floor possessed a peculiar remoteness. It was an old building and the walls were thick. There was nobody else on the third floor; apparently most of the visitors had been discouraged by the first and second floors. Most men, Elaine was aware, went to picture galleries only in the hope of seeing enticing pictures of nude women; and most women went to picture galleries in the hope of seeing "cultural" exhibits, which they could later—to prove their superiority—report having seen.

There were pictures of nude women in the museum, but they had no sex appeal; and there were no exhibits in the building upon which bourgeoise women could report at bridge clubs and receive recognition of superiority from their envious associates.

Miriam noticed her hypercritical attitude and remarked a trifle coolly:

"You're out of sorts today, Elaine."

"I'm afraid I am."

"Rather go somewhere else?"

"No, I wouldn't have missed this. I'm surprised that you haven't brought me here before … how many other interesting things are you saving to show me when you get around to it?"

For some reason this made Miriam feel sad.

"A world of things, Elaine; but you're losing sympathy with me … you're losing sympathy with me and my ideals."

"Am I?" Elaine asked it in a tone of voice which indicated that she was interrogating herself as well as Miriam.

"Yes, you are," Miriam affirmed somewhat crossly.

"Did I used to be different?"

"Very, Elaine."

"How?"

"… Well, more sympathetic toward—toward things like *this*. Of late you're contemptuous of anything that doesn't smack of the comfortably bourgeoisie."

"You're being nasty, Miriam."

"I'm being truthful."

There was a heavy red carpet upon the floor. It completely deadened the sound of their steps. They moved slowly across the room. Separated by several feet. Elaine went to a window and gazed into the street. She felt heartened by what she saw. Automobiles precisely suited to their purposes, the lines of their construction expressing a utilitarian practicality that was restful. Given a chance to design automobiles, what on earth might these artists who had filled the museum with their queer pictures do? Miriam stood beside her. It was late afternoon.

"You're drifting away from me, Elaine. Even now, during those periods when you used to be closest to me I feel that I'm losing you."

"What makes you think so, Miriam?"

"You're changing in some permanent way."

"I don't feel it greatly, although I do think I have an idea what you mean."

"You're changing because you're *really* falling in love in the most disgustingly conventional manner."

"With whom?"

"Hyde...."

"You must be wrong, Miriam; if he were to suddenly appear here now my own feeling would be one of annoyance, and I'd want to get away from him as soon as possible."

"Nevertheless, Elaine, you're changing radically. Do you know why you feel out of sympathy now with such things as these exhibits here? It's because you no longer feel handicapped or afraid. It's the souls at bay who like to be around such things as these pictures. They remind them of the fact that there are many others on the defensive and unadjusted to life."

"Surely that's not why *you*...." Elaine began; Miriam cut in with:

"Yes, that's why; I might as well confess it."

"But you've been so confident right along. You've been—"

"Whistling in the dark, Elaine. That's what all of us cold ones do.... That's why we're eternally insisting upon our own superiority, through making fun of the normal ones ... we have to keep insisting ... otherwise we couldn't believe it ourselves."

"You're morbid today, Miriam."

"Yes, because I have a premonition that you and I are not going to be together much longer."

"Well, you're very much mistaken in that."

"I hope so, Elaine, but...."

"Suppose, Miriam, that I *do* care a bit more for Hyde than I used to. What does that signify? Don't lots of women, with husbands and lovers...."

"Yes, I know all that, Elaine ... but I'm not sure that I ought to exert myself to win you completely away from that even if I could."

"You don't have to exert yourself."

"I might do it without intending to."

"What do you mean?"

"I don't know, Elaine; life is very strange. I used to be sure of at least one thing ... now I'm not even confident of that any more. I used to be sure of what would give me happiness—now I don't know."

"You're making much out of nothing. You feel blue today, that's all; you'll be all over it tomorrow."

"Yes, I do feel blue.... I'm blue because your attitude here confirms what I suspected; that you're losing sympathy with.... Oh ... everything that I represent. Not that I'd want your sympathy.... You're like a patient who had been for a time convalescing in a hospital. While you were ill you loved those around you who were also ill; most of them, perhaps, more so than yourself. And when you got well and left you said to yourself that you would never forget those others who had been in the hospital with you ... that you'd never forget the suffering and the helplessness of those others.

"Then you recovered and got out.... And went back a time or two; but when you were completely well again you found that you were made uncomfortable by the sight of sick people, and finally you made no returns to visit them."

"But you've always said, Miriam, that it wasn't a question of inferiority, or of—"

"Oh yes, I know ... I said a lot. But the fact remains that your association with me made you weaker; while your association with Hyde has made you in some way stronger, more able to face life in a robust way."

"Miriam, I'm amazed to hear you admit such things; it completely refutes everything you've...."

"Yes, I know, but somehow I feel the approach of something that will undo ... well, everything I stand for. Perhaps it would be best to ... set you free."

" 'Set me free?' "

"If I can."

"But I don't *want* to be free."

"I know, Elaine; like everyone else you want to both have your cake and eat it. Of course it can't be done."

"Nonsense, it can be done. It's all perfectly simple, Miriam; I don't know why you make such a complicated thing of it all today. In one mood I prefer Hyde; in another I prefer your company. What's so damnably complicated about that?"

"Just this, I am afraid, Elaine: When you are in the mood for Hyde, you are yourself; when you are in the mood for me you are under some sort of spell which I seem in some manner to create. Before, there was some need for all that, a purpose which even you know nothing about. And now, fate has made a mockery of it all."

"Stop it, Miriam; you make my blood run cold." She looked around at the walls and shuddered. "Let's get out of here, for goodness' sake. It's this place that's having such an awful effect upon us. These pictures! ... It is as though cripples were hanged there, demanding sympathy and attention for their infirmities; cursing those who withhold it ... calling them stupid and bourgeoisie and...."

"It is a lot like that, Elaine.... These cripples, who turn to the arts. I've seen enough of it to understand.... The writers of purple novels who invariably have around them groups of young men or young women whom they in some way succeed in crippling like themselves, so that they can feed upon them.

"... The poets who write unintelligibly and who inevitably attract to them other weak ones whom they render weaker, and who enter the incurable wards of life with them, and never leave the wards.... In time become confirmed cripples themselves and in turn cast their dark spells over others.

"... The painters who create misshapen pictures, interpreting life in disordered terms ... whenever you visit their studios you find a coterie of those who are subtly being remolded by the 'master'.... The master who knows that—since they are really weaker than he, in that they cannot create anything at all—they will at last become objects so pitiable as to distract his attention from his own infirmities and permit him to have for companionship someone toward whom he can feel a superiority that will hearten him.

"... These eccentric sculptors, with their creations that are meaningless, and yet which express an impression of objectified unhealthiness. I know several of them; always there are those they have attracted to them, in some sinister way; those whom they are molding and shaping even more directly than the clay or marble that they work with.

"... I mustn't do that to you, Elaine—and yet I *would,* if it had any meaning or justification. But I'm convinced at last that it hasn't. You're too strong for me after all; and so, you see, I make a virtue of my failure."

"Come down to earth, Miriam; there's no way that you could get rid of me, even if you wanted to. It's true that there will probably continue to be times when I shall desert you for awhile ... but I'll be back. I'll return whether you want me to or not ... and there's certainly nothing that you can do about it."

"If I were only sure, Elaine, that you returned because you *wanted* to."

"What possible evidence is there to the contrary?"

"I don't know ... but these writers and artists and sculptors I've been talking about ... and even the bizarre musicians ... all those creative ones, with their intensely powerful, if distorted minds.... The influence they seem to exert over their proteges ... smacks ... if you examine it very closely ... of some form of hypnotic control."

"Don't be melodramatic, Miriam."

"Do you mean to tell me, Elaine, that you haven't already thought of that ... both Hyde and you?"

Elaine did not reply. Finally she tugged at Miriam's arm.

"Come, for God's sake, Miriam, let's get out of this psychopathic place before we get any nuttier than we are already."

# CHAPTER TWENTY-FOUR

## *HYDE AND ELAINE ELOPE*

HYDE WAS in the side yard knocking golf balls around. He was in no very good humor. The sod was new, and it had not yet integrated where slabs of it had been laid down by the landscape gardener. The little white ball took a most erratic course over it. Nothing, he reflected with bitterness, was right about his God-damned house. Nothing! He was particularly aggrieved over the fact today because he could have felt splendidly. He was experiencing one of those now, to him, periodical returns to a state of decency. Forgotten, for the time being, were the pleasures of the flesh. He was thinking of the golf season to come. He speculated concerning his wife's present whereabouts. Usually, when he had one of those returns to a placid state of mind she appeared almost immediately. But he sighed in resignation. Even if she did appear it wouldn't really mean anything. They'd be great pals for a few days, and then she would relapse, and he would. He was sick and tired of it all. Viciously he drove at the ball. It lifted into the air, when the club met it with a sound and solidly satisfying crack, and soared away out of sight.

He walked toward the house. A car turned in at the private driveway. He looked toward it. It was the Packard. George was at the wheel. Miriam and Elaine, he supposed; he'd have to be getting on somewhere.... Into town, though there was nothing he could think of that he wanted to do. In town uniformed policemen hustled the crowds along with a gruff "Keep moving." … And to the more comfortably situated souls like himself some cosmic policeman gave continually the same injunction: "Keep moving." … To where? To what? he asked himself angrily as the car drove up and stopped.

Elaine got out of the car. She was alone. She hurried to his side:

"How do you feel?" she inquired anxiously.

"First rate," Hyde told her. "Where's Miriam?"

"Sick, Hyde."

"She would be. The only time I ever feel well is when she's sick, poor girl. What ails her now? Why doesn't she have a baby? That might give us nine months of respite."

"She's got another one of her migraine attacks. Oh, Hyde … I—" He waited but she did not go on. He prompted.

"Yes, what is it, Elaine?"

"Hyde, do you think—but then it's too mad. I can't make sense of it myself, only—"

"Well, anyway," he concluded, when she could not finish coherently, "we'll have a few days of peace and each other's companionship. I suppose that's all we're to expect out of our married life."

"Come into the house, Hyde; I want to talk to you. I've got an idea, but I haven't got the nerve to spring it on you all at once. I'm afraid you'll think I am crazy."

"*I* think *you're* crazy, Elaine, after the things I've—especially the other day when.…"

"That wasn't you, Hyde."

"*What* wasn't me?"

"Come inside."

He followed her into the house. She hurried upstairs to her room and he trailed along mystified. When they had reached the room she closed the door. Asked him to sit down. Seated herself opposite.

"Hyde, I'm convinced that Miriam has some weird influence over both of us."

"But Elaine, she's—"

"Yes, I know. But something has a strange influence over her, and she passes it on to us."

"But how *could* she, Elaine?"

"I don't know; and I'm not even sure she does it intentionally. I think, now, that even she suspects that she does have a strange influence over us. Just now, when the attack came on her she said wearily:

" 'All right, you and Hyde can be yourselves for a few days.' She said it bitterly, and sadly, as though she knew that she was ruining our lives without reason or excuse."

"I'm afraid, Elaine, that I don't follow you at all."

"No, I knew you wouldn't; I can't quite follow the idea myself. But I feel the truth of it just the same. You and I are trained to explain everything in logical terms. When we come up against a situation we can't explain in logical terms our academic training leads us to deny the very existence of it. That's rot, and you know it. If people had acted that way in the early centuries nobody would have learned anything. We're up against something that can't be explained academically.... Yet it's *there* just the same. I *know* it."

He nodded gravely.

"I'm inclined to agree with you, to a certain extent; but I'd be more likely to put it down to our own natural cussedness, than to the influence of some third party. Human beings, you know, are always prone to blame their deficiencies on somebody else."

"Yes, I know, but—Hyde, I'm *convinced* that you and I could be happy together."

He shook his head sadly.

"Oh yes we could, Hyde. On each one of these occasions when we've come back to ourselves we've been closer to each other, learned each time to care a little more. I'm *sure* of it."

"I'm sure of that part of it too, Elaine. There are times when I do love you sincerely and deeply—but I've burned too many of the possible bridges between us by my lamentable conduct when—"

"No you haven't."

"Do you mean to say, Elaine, that you could *ever* have the slightest respect or real affection for me after—"

"Hyde, there are times when I see a duality of character in you so clearly that I am almost frightened.... And, thus clearly seeing it, I never attach to the best *you* the actions of the other you.... Those things—that you're thinking of—belong to one person—and the other things ... the times when you're sweet and thoughtful and dear ... then you're the other person, and in my own mind I see no connection between the two persons at all."

"But what are we to do, Elaine?" He threw out his hands helplessly.

"What would *you* suggest, Hyde?"

"I think the only sensible solution is divorce or separation."

"But I don't want to divorce you, Hyde, or to separate from you."

"Or I, Elaine but—!"

"Do you want me to make a suggestion, Hyde?"

"*Do!*"

"Let's go abroad.... We could go to France and see if by escaping from her influence—"

"Do you mean to say you'd be willing to go away without her? ... You weren't willing before."

"Yes, I know … and I won't be if—Oh, Hyde, let's hurry. Let's run like the devil immediately. Let's take a slow boat, so that if I change my mind we'll be out there on the water, and there'll be nothing I can do about it, at least for a time.… Then, if our experiment doesn't work, we can be divorced in Paris and return … and if it does work—!"

"It won't work, Elaine. We wouldn't be running away from anything. We'd be taking it right along with us because it's inside ourselves, don't you see?"

"I can see that you're speaking logically … but logic … that's one of the toys of schoolmasters … and see what shape the world's in today after years of playing with such futile toys. Intuition … even if it is ruled out of all the best classrooms, it's—"

He smiled wryly.

"After all, honey, what you're suggesting appeals to me *thoroughly*. At worst, so far as I am concerned, I'll have you all to myself for some days … and it's wonderful to have you to myself when you're in the sort of mood you are in now. But when your mood passes—it's going to be hell on you."

"I'm willing to take the chance, Hyde. I do love you. I do want you. I want you to make me be what I ought to be.… Keep me from eventually turning into a horribly twisted thing that—"

"I have no such powers as that, Elaine."

"Oh, please, take me into your arms. I'm so frightened, and so—I feel so queer—to change completely this way, and feel, too, that at any minute I may change again and—Oh! I can't stand it any more, Hyde. Please help me. You're such a dear when you want to be."

Rising he went over to her chair, picked her up bodily and sat down with her in his lap. Gently he kissed her, held her tight. Like a tired, frightened little girl she put her head down upon his shoulder and curved a shapely arm around his neck.

"Listen, sweet," he said; "if you're perfectly sure you want to make the experiment I'll do it."

"Oh do, quickly, before I can change my mind."

Rising again, he put her down and stepped to the 'phone. Dialed the number of a prominent travel agency.

"Is there a boat leaving for France *tonight?*" he asked, when the connection had been made.

They packed quickly and joyously, like children heading for summer camp. When the preparations were nearly complete, Elaine thought of Miriam; sick, miserable, and alone. The thought filled her with pity and regret. She picked up her 'phone and dialed resolutely.

"Hello," Miriam said dully.

"Hello, Miriam, this is Elaine. Hyde and I are leaving for Europe tonight and I wanted to say goodbye."

Miriam realized that she ought to care terribly about this, but now, nothing mattered. Great waves of pain kept sweeping in and dulling her emotions.

"I suppose you realize what will probably happen?"

"It won't, Miriam, Hyde has completely changed, and so have I. We're very happy. And do you know what else I've decided? Hyde hates Winton Hall and so do I. When we return from Europe I'm going to have it torn down and we'll build over again."

Vaguely, off in the remote outer spaces, Miriam imagined that she heard the dull, dead crack of Doom.

# CHAPTER TWENTY-FIVE
## *HIRTATION ON THE HIGH SEAS*

S HE WAS going across, she said, to try to get into French motion pictures. They'd somehow met at luncheon. Hyde held her close, as they danced after dinner.

She was nearly a head shorter than he, with huge brown eyes, and a baby manner which made him sincerely believe that she was no more than the nineteen she claimed. Her hair would have been straight, he knew, had she not provided herself with a permanent; but it was a most effective permanent, and he was constrained to admit that it added to her total effectiveness; which was decidedly compelling.

"Let's go out and cool off a bit," he suggested.

They walked out upon one of the lower decks and stood in the lee of the wind.

"You French?" he asked.

"Half.... My mother. I was born in France, but we came to America when I was twelve."

"Folks living?"

"Yep. Dad works for Ford, out at the River Rouge Plant. He's a night foreman."

"... And you're going to France to be a motion picture actress! Why not to Hollywood?"

"Because I wouldn't have the chance in Hollywood I'll have in France. I know some people over there."

"Won't it cost a lot of money?"

"Plenty ... but it's a sort of investment. I'm the only child. Dad makes pretty fair money, even now. He used to make a lot of money. He saved it up and invested it and lost it all. Now he doesn't save any more. Not like he used to anyway. He saved up enough for me to take this trip."

"Your Dad's no fool," Hyde approved. "I'd consider you a far better investment than the slips of paper investment bankers sell."

"You think I'll get on?"

"You bet," he said sincerely. "You've good features, and an excellent speaking voice—and you're popping over with personality.... Yes, you'll get on, no doubt about it."

She stared up at him speculatively out of her large, dark eyes. There was an uncertain light coming from a port hole which opened into one of the salons. He saw that she was debating something with herself. She was youthful and piquant. The cuddly sort who expressed sex appeal in every curve and posture.

"If I had better clothes ..." she mourned. "He couldn't afford as much for clothes as I'd have liked to have."

"Clothes *are* important, I suppose," Hyde remarked guardedly. Did he, he mused, want this little thing? He knew that he did. All the time he had been dancing with her he had been wanting her; and she was the sort of young imp who danced close and made one conscious of her desirability. Putting his arm carelessly around her he bent over and kissed her. Her mouth was small, and warm and slightly damp. When she did not object he kissed her again, lingeringly. Passion flooded through him.

"Oh!" she objected, pushing him away, "what if your wife should come out here?"

"It wouldn't make any difference," he said easily. "And, besides, she won't. She's busy with two prospects herself; that young fellow from Harvard, and that very formidable Miss Hanchett."

"You mean the woman with the two Chinese manservants?"

"Yes."

"I never heard such wild, outspoken sex talk in all my life as I did from that woman. I met her at the rail as the boat was leaving the harbor, and until I heard all of her quaint notions, I thought she was queer and was trying to make me."

"She's a poet and a notorious sensualist. She's famous for her ... shall we say spectacular(?) parties."

"Oh yeh?"

"Yes, really; I know she's a poet—and a good one. Surely you've heard of Mamba Hanchett?"

"Nope, I never heard of her; I never read poetry. Is it a good racket?"

"Poetry? I should say not. She doesn't make a living out of it; she has money."

"She *has!*" the little French girl appeared to be deeply shocked and chagrined; Hyde chuckled; added:

"... So, you see, you mercenary little creature, you made a bad mistake."

She tried to look offended; but giggled in the middle of it.

"Yes," she finally said; "I sure did. But the way she dresses you wouldn't think she had a dime, would you?"

"Oh, I don't know about that," Hyde observed. He was surprised that he was not offended at her grossly material attitude; in most women it would completely have destroyed any feeling of desirability, were it injected into the situation so early and with such bleak cynicism; but with this little thing somehow her naïvete glossed it over.

"I have been known to buy a dress occasionally myself," he informed her.

She glanced up at him guardedly.

"... But you're young, and handsome yourself, and you've got a lovely wife—you could get any girl. I didn't let you flirt with me because I had any intention of letting you go any farther ... I let you pick me up because I liked you and wanted to dance with you."

"That's terrifically complimentary," he let his tone carry notice of his unbelief.

They could hear the music from the ballroom very clearly. Along the lower deck at intervals there were other couples making bedroom arrangements for the evening.

"You don't believe me, do you," she charged. "... Well, it's true. I'm not taking any chances. I never took any chances. I'm a virgin."

Reaching down he took her hand and shook it.

"Congratulations, my dear.... And from Detroit! It's almost unbelievable."

"It was pretty hard," she confided. "And I don't mean I've never had any experiences; I have had—but always with different kinds of men than you are. Men who weren't attractive and couldn't usually get girls. When my father was fairly well off I went to a private school for girls; and had everything I wanted. Then when he got laid off for a while, and before he got to work again for less money, there was a time when we had to go awfully easy on expenses. I was young and pretty and I wanted nice clothes so I put my private school education to some practical use—no—not what you're thinking, either. I wouldn't do that for anything."

"I understand," he assured her, "perfectly."

"But you don't believe me?"

"Oh yes I do."

"I *am* innocent and I can prove it."

"I don't doubt it."

"… So you see, Mister, you and I can't be playmates."

"Why can't we?"

He could have kicked himself, but he desired her madly.… On any terms. The fragrance of her young womanhood; the softness and naïvete of her. The sheer attraction of what she was suggesting.

"You're not just saying that so you can get me alone and then—"

"Do I appear to be the sort who would pull any rough stuff?"

"No, you don't."

She put a key into his hands.

"I left the door unlocked. I can get in. Come on down in about ten or fifteen minutes, so I'll have time to get fixed up. Are you sure that your wife—"

"… She wouldn't interfere in any way even if she knew all about it."

"All right, then—but no rough stuff—promise?"

"I promise."

And then she was gone; leaving the heat of her warm young person upon him. He remembered the immaturity of her breasts; the youthful narrowness of her hips … her lithe slimness.

… But without her bright person present to force all coherent thought from his mind, he was instantly provided with doubts.

It hadn't then been Miriam, he decided. It had, of course, been absurd to blame Miriam. A phantasy which now that he scrutinized it in the cold light of reason had been preposterous from the start. Miriam had nothing to do with his and Elaine's wanderings. Here he was hundreds of miles away from her; completely cut off from her, and the same old leit motif was singing itself over and over in his mind.... And Heaven only knew to what end. All of the time he had been talking to the little French child he had been conscious of clipping his words short; making his sentences brief, so that he would not run into the queer physiological-psychological affection which had of late been increasingly bothering him, so that he was deathly afraid that he might become permanently a stammerer, could he not wean himself from the things which so sharply upset his nervous system and exhausted his nervous vitality.

Back there across the dark miles of water toward which he now turned his gaze was Miriam. Alone and deserted; on the outlandishly idiotic theory that she was some sort of witch. And she was blameless. He was the one at fault. Elaine and he. He cursed himself for a morbid fool in the dark; then glanced anxiously at his watch. Only a few minutes had passed.

He went impatiently into the ballroom, thinking that within the span of his memory time had never before passed so slowly.

He saw Elaine seated at a table with Miss Hanchett and the young fellow from Harvard, and from the incredulous, almost alarmed look he had on his face, Hyde could tell that plans were already being made for the evening's entertainment. With Miss Hanchett presiding, Hyde felt sure that Elaine would be treated to a spectacle that would fulfill even her wildest dreams.

Again and again he jerked out his watch and impatiently examined it. He watched the second hand for a moment, to be sure that the watch was running. Tarried on one of the lower decks to watch a game the passengers were playing by electric light out on the open deck.

At last, after a final glance at his watch he descended still another stairway to a lower deck, and started scrutinizing the numbers upon stateroom doors. At last he found the right one, using the tag on the key to guide him. He knocked softly. There was an instant "Come in," that sounded distinctly through the ventilator section of the door. Entering he found the stateroom in darkness.

Almost immediately the light was snapped on.

"I just wanted to be sure it was you," she explained. She was sitting upon the edge of the bed, holding a scarf over her loveliness. Her body was fresh and pinkish and glowing from, evidently, a shower just taken. He went over and sat down beside her. Took her into his arms. She lifted her lips. He clamped his mouth over them. One of his hands wandered. She did not object. He gently bent her back. She relinquished the scarf. She was youthful and sweet.

# CHAPTER TWENTY-SIX
## *HAMES OF PASSION*

THERE WAS a strong wind blowing. For once the strangely protected pocket of land in which the house stood had gotten itself directly into a gale. The usually stiff and erect poplars were swaying wildly in the gale. Miriam was for a moment startled. She had never before seen the trees move. As she got down out of the car it appeared to her that they waved some sort of grim welcome.

She stood for a moment indecisive, afraid; a slender figure against the ravishing wind which tore at her skirts. Max sat imperturbably at the wheel, staring straight ahead.

"Wait," she said crisply, and moved toward the house, the wind almost blowing her over. There was the first real summer storm of the season blowing up. Far out over the ocean black clouds were piled up, and against them bright flashes of lightning shone, though the storm was as yet so far away that the thunder could not be heard.

Letting herself in with a passkey, Miriam walked through the house; dialed the garage. There was no answer. There was nobody on the grounds. The servants, she knew, had been divided between Elaine's and Hyde's parents—they were to come over once a week to keep things in order.

Assured that there was nobody in the house, Miriam went back to the car.

"You may go, Max. Return home. If mother asks don't tell her I am here. I shall call home for the car when I am ready to leave; but if you're out I can 'phone the village for a taxi."

"Yes, Miss," he said imperturbably, and drove off. She watched the car until it turned into the trunk road. It wasn't possible, she told herself, that once she had been held in her chauffeur's arms. It must have been one of her mad dreams, she decided; though she knew, well enough, that it had not been a dream.

When Max had gone she went back into the house; walked through it and continued on to the garage. She had a full set of keys, including the garage keys.

In the garage she found numerous small and large cans filled with various types of oils. These she carried into the house, emptying their contents everywhere. When the small cans gave out she found a bucket and pumped sufficient gasoline from the tank beneath the garage to fill the bucket a dozen times. She poured the contents of the bucket, after each trip out to the garage, in a different place throughout the house. The reek of oil and gasoline was nauseating. Though it was chilly out, she opened most of the windows.

The hard labor of carrying the heavy buckets of gasoline from the garage to the house kept her from thinking.... But, this labor ended, thought seized upon her. Her mind darted madly in every direction, seeking escape. The storm was coming closer, and the wind was increasing. There was a low roll of thunder in the distance, following a sharp bolt of lightning which, in the late afternoon cloud-inculcated gloom seemed to be of an unearthly consistency.

Going to Elaine's room she shut the door and took from a closet a suitcase which she had put there the day before. Working hurriedly she emptied the contents of the suitcase upon the floor. Among the things contained in it was a long, slim dagger whose bright blade presently shone out menacingly as another bolt of lighting lit up the room.

Working swiftly she divested herself of her clothing and stood for a moment slim and straight and white in the semi dark of the room. There was another lightning flash, this time a ruddy one, that touched her superb body for a moment with rubric. As the lightning flashed she caught a very distinct glimpse of herself in the mirror and was deeply shocked. The effect of the lightning had been to sharpen and accentuate her perfect features in an unpleasant, frightening way.

For a moment ungovernable fear shook her. She stood very still, wondering if, after all, she would have the courage.... But she *must* have, she told herself firmly.

There was nothing left now. Hyde and Elaine were drawing together again, eluding her frantic impediments, compelled by a love that was growing stronger than even her own strange powers. The thought of their returning, of being forced to watch Winton Hall being rent and torn asunder was more than she could bear. She was fully aware that only animal courage had brought her through the last attack, and that the next would mean her doom. With a grim earnestness, she had sworn that this great house would pass from existence with her in one final burst of flame and brilliance, defiant of life in all its cold, tawdry dullness.

She dressed with meticulous care, scenting her body with the most costly and exquisite fragrances on Elaine's dressing table. Finally, she draped her lovely body with a magnificent gown of black velvet, whose neckline delved deeply into the enticing cleft between her swelling breasts. The dress was garnished with a tremendous serpent, embroidered in gold, who twined his glistening length upward from the hem and around her torso several times, with the head poised as if to sink its fangs into her soft bosom. It was a striking creation, displaying her superb contours

JACK WOODFORD

to the maximum possible advantage. Miriam had bought it especially for this occasion.

With calm resolution, she picked up the dagger and left the room. She walked regally through the hall, touching the teakwood tables and marble busts that flanked its walls with gentle tenderness. She turned on the main switch at the top of the huge staircase, and the entire house was immediately bathed in the dazzling flood of light that flowed from the crystal chandeliers.

Looking out over the great entrance hall, Miriam visualized a great party in progress. The halls rang with female laughter and resonant male voices. Scores of admiring and envious eyes were upon her as she descended the marble stairs with an air of austere majesty. She entered the main dining hall followed by a ghostly company of society's elite; fawning, scraping, begging for her favor. She placed a record of a Viennese waltz on the luxurious phonograph which stood in the corner, set the needle in the fleeting groove, and walked to the huge banquet table which she had ordered fully set two days before. With extreme care, she lit the thirty-six tapers which adorned it, with wooden matches from a small gold box which she carried in the pocket of her gown, cautiously placing the burned match-sticks where they could not fall on the gasoline-soaked rug. Then with queenly dignity, she walked to the head of the great table, and stared thoughtfully down its imposing length. She imagined two endless rows of faces; the rich, the talented, whose eyes all paid her homage. Then, with an almost mechanical precision, Miriam took the final match from the glittering box, struck it, and allowed it to drop to the floor.

The sudden roar of the flames surprised her. They leaped up with a vengeful, savage fury. To Miriam, the flames possessed a fire and brilliance worthy of this historic evening, when she was giving her first and last great party at Winton Hall.

At last, with the flames raging on all sides, she grasped the top of her dress and ripped it down to the waist.

For a moment she felt with her hand, beneath the firm rounded warmth of her left breast. Easy enough it was to locate her heart. It was pounding mightily. Taking up the slim dagger she poised it perfectly, then, with both hands upon its hilt, while the phonograph played Vienna Blood, plunged the slim bright steel into her heart.

# CHAPTER TWENTY-SEVEN
## *IN EACH OTHER'S ARMS*

HYDE WENT to the rail and stood gazing out over the water. Something had happened to him. Something tremendous. He could not imagine what it might be. There was a crepuscular light over the sea. Far off at the horizon he could see faintly the lights of another ship nearing them.

The indistinct light made sky and sea blend together. The movement of the ship was soundless and noiseless. It was as though the vessel hung suspended between sky and sea.

Below decks he could hear the orchestra in the dining room playing. The deck was deserted, except for a solitary seaman who stalked around on watch.

He felt an overwhelming desire to see Elaine.... Speculated as to where she might be at the moment, and what she might be doing. He wanted to see her because he wished to acquaint her with the fact that a tremendous change had come over him. Yet, soberly considering, he saw that it would be quite silly to rush up to her and say: "Elaine, I'm changed in some fundamental way." She'd be sure to think he had taken leave of his senses. Probably be amused at him.

... And, besides, he was fairly sure that he knew where she was at the moment.... Probably in Miss Hanchett's stateroom, listening to that lady expound her endless illogical, but nevertheless brilliantly plausible, views upon life.

He sighed deeply. It would not be possible, he felt, for Elaine and him to go on as they had been. If he cared less for her it would be easy enough ... but the time had come, he knew, when he could no longer share her with anyone gracefully.

There was, he saw, only one logical thing left. Divorce. He must divorce her, or permit her to divorce him, in Paris. It could be easily enough arranged. In melancholy vein he thought of how, just shortly before the wedding, he had considered with alarm the likelihood of divorce; viewed it as a major catastrophe ... and now the certainty of it was upon them.... And afterward—what to do would be a problem. He knew that the sudden and deeply radical change which had come over him was no fanciful one. It was real. Terribly so. The salt, he knew, of sexual promiscuity, had forever lost its savor. It could mean nothing any more unless the person involved meant something beyond a soft body. And it was impossible to imagine anyone but Elaine meaning anything in that way.

Then what ... ? Roaming around the world? That was a bore and a nuisance. Return? Entry into business affairs, in preparation for taking over his father's interests when that gentleman should die? He shuddered with a feeling of intolerable boredom. Nothing could be more stupid than guarding a two-generation-old hoard of money. That was a business for unimaginative, stolid men, hypnotized by the thought of material value. If only Elaine were different, it would all be so simple. Not money, time, place, condition of life would matter anything if Elaine ... they might be penniless together ... yet the fact that they *were* together.... But they could not ever be *really* together, he was sure. Glancing directly down he tried to see the water below. He could not. The light had faded. Were he to drop down into that vague space it would be like falling into blankness. Yet the thought of suicide was peculiarly repugnant at the moment. He wanted to live—to live with the new feeling of lift that had come to him. Yet there was nothing to live for, really, he assured himself.

He was aware of someone near him. He could not have told why he was aware, because he had heard nothing ... felt nothing—unless the lower depths of his mind with their keener appreciation had detected a sound or felt the vibration of steps upon the steel deck.

"Oh! Here you are!" Elaine's voice sounded at his side. Turning, he found her close to him.

"I've been hunting everywhere for you," she said.

"Searching for *me!* I thought you would have gone into one of your sessions with Miss Hanchett?" He did not say it bitterly, or with rebuke; but sadly.

"She's a nasty old snake, Hyde."

"What!" he echoed and turned around in surprise to try to see her face. He could see only a soft white blur near to him; a cloud had passed over the surface of the moon and temporarily deepened the dark. Far above them the small red and white lights on the ship's radio aerial pricked the heavy back drop of night. As the wind changed slightly a fine spray released by steam floating from one of the stacks fell about them.

"Hyde, I suppose you'll think I'm crazy, but just a short while ago something happened to me. Something strange, but beautiful; and very, very real, even if I can't give you the faintest idea as to what it was."

He trembled in eagerness. Tried to find the proper words to say to her what he wished to, but he could not find words. He replied merely:

"Yes, I know what you mean; I felt it too."

"You did!"

"Yes."

"What do you suppose it means, Hyde?"

"I haven't the faintest idea."

"The nearest I can come to describing it, Hyde, is that I feel as I did years ago; before I ever went to college. I feel as though ... you know I often talk about 'brightnesses' ... that's because my grandmother ... used to tell me things ... made everything seem ... well, anyway, I feel as though I had come out of some sort of shadow that had been over me for several years ... as though I were about to find some of those brightnesses. And *this time* I feel, as I never before felt, that the change is going to be permanent."

"You've come nearer to describing the way I feel than I could have, Elaine. And I, too, know that the change is a permanent one. It's like the peculiar change that used to come over us when Miriam was ill; only this time it's ten times stronger, and I have that absolute conviction that it's to be permanent.... And I feel hideously tired, as though I had been struggling against something, and had at last overthrown it, but had all but worn myself out in the process."

"Exactly," she concurred. "That's precisely the way I feel. I'd like to lie down and close my eyes and sleep for hours and hours ... but I didn't want to go to my stateroom alone. Would you mind coming down with me?"

She had spoken like a child. He put his arm tenderly around her and kissed her.

Together they went below. The dance orchestra in the dining room was going full blast now; but they had no desire tonight to dance. Their limbs felt heavy and tired. Unlocking the door to their suite he stood aside for her to enter.

Grasping his hand she pulled him into her bedroom.

"Don't leave me for awhile, Hyde; I have the most peculiar feeling that I had lost you, and just found you, and that you might get lost again. Are you really going to bed?"

"If you don't mind; I'm feeling more tired every minute. I don't know what's come over me."

"So do I. Do you mind sleeping in here with me tonight? I'm sort of … afraid … I don't know what of, only …"

He helped her to undress. Brought her bed pyjamas. Then disrobed himself. Climbed in with her. They turned out the lights. She snuggled dose to him, and one of her small hands found its way into his. Never had he felt so tender toward her. She whispered:

"Hyde, you remember once we talked about having a baby? … And you took it for granted that I wouldn't ever want one?" When he was silent she went on: "I *would* like to have one, Hyde … now. I'd love to have your baby. I wouldn't be afraid at all—If you really loved me—and somehow I feel that you really do—now."

Such a wave of tenderness came over him that he could hardly speak.

"It would be wonderful," he whispered; "only, I'd be afraid for you … until I can understand what it is that's happened to us tonight. I might change again, and—"

"You don't think I'll change again, Hyde?"

"If you do, I can't bear it this time."

"Oh, I won't change. I promise you I won't."

Her hand in his, she lay silent, a trifle uneasy, but a lot happy. Gradually her tired mind, which seemed just to have finished some sort of tremendous struggle, slipped off into unconsciousness.

Some time later the telephone rang. Hyde and Elaine jerked and sat up in a daze. So deeply had they been sleeping that the 'phone rang "again and again insistently before Hyde summoned the wits to reach out and take it up from the stand by the side of the bed.

"Hello?" he managed thickly. The ship's operator said:

"New York *Daily Standard* calling you from shore, sir, over the wireless 'phone."

"Yes?" Hyde murmured, still not fully awake.

A new voice came on, after a moment of mysterious whirrings.

"This Mr. Hyde Winton speaking?" the newspaper man inquired from shore.

A picture came to Hyde's mind of the small white and red lights at the foremast, marking the ship's radio aerial.

"Yes, this is Hyde Winton."

"Mr. Winton, your home has been completely destroyed by fire. The servants were away. Miss Miriam Atwell was burned with the house. The firemen report that she had killed herself shortly before the house burned. Can you give us any reason for her suicide?"

"Yes," Hyde replied, thoroughly awake now. "She was in bad health. She suffered devastating migraine attacks which made her life miserable. It might also be well to bear in mind, young man, that libel actions can be brought in criminal courts as well as in civil courts. It might also be well to not forget in this connection that my father is a fairly wealthy and influential man."

"I get you," the news man chuckled. "I won't make any cracks. Migraine it is—and you don't need to worry, Mr. Winton."

"It's Miriam," Elaine declared. "She's killed herself."

"Yes," he confirmed gravely. "Poor little thing—maybe, at that, it was best."

"Poor Miriam...." Elaine seconded. "Still—it was almost the only way out for her."

Her hand stole into his again. She said with awe:

"The radio telephone is certainly a marvelous thing ... here we are on a boat ... and some newspaper man at a desk back in New York—"

He put his arms around her. Again he inwardly saw the red light and the white light on the tip ends of the small boom which supported the radio aerial.

"I know something that beats the radio hollow, Elaine. You and I somehow knew that Miriam was dead several hours ago.... But we better never tell anybody our strange experience. They'd think we were crazy."

"It's all so weird," she said in a low tone; "don't let's think about it any more."

"No, let's not, honey—and, by the way, I'm not so tired now, are you?"

"No, Hyde, I feel—" her eyes gleamed up at him.

"Oh! ... You *do!*" he teased, and took her with masterful intentness into his strong arms.

THE END

www.ingramcontent.com/pod-product-compliance
Lightning Source LLC
Chambersburg PA
CBHW030120260626
47156CB00008B/2735